Passages from Rolfe Humphries' translation of The Satires of Juvenal are quoted by permission of Indiana University Press.

The op-ed piece in Chapter 9 appeared originally in *The Atlanta Journal-Constitution*.

Chapter 1, in a slightly different form, was published as "Won't You Come Home, Bill Bailey?" by *Press* magazine.

Printed in the Canada

ISBN 1-930180-09-8

Published by GLAD DAY BOOKS
P.O. Box 699
Enfield, NH 03748
1-888-874-6904 toll free

Library of Congress Cataloging in Publication Data:

Gallant, James, 1937-
    The Big Bust at Tyrone's Rooming House
    A Glad Day Book

The Big Bust at Tyrone's Rooming House

A Novel of Atlanta

James Gallant

Editor's Preface

The aim of Glad Day Books has been to bridge the gap between works of imaginative literature and articles of political theory and criticism. This book, *Big Bus at Tyrone's Rooming House,* fits that description. Though it's about rogues and a story of an inner city neighborhood in the throes of gentrification, it has a wider perspective: this is the desperate economics of the poor, the hopelessness of the police and the blandness of higher officials.

That said, the editors have had serious concerns about how the book might be received. It is bound to offend some readers. Is it the language, southern black speech? The narrative point of view? Is it condescending? Are the narrator's observations self-serving? In the end, it is the ideology of the gentry, rather than the resisters of gentrification. Or is it undermined by laughter?

The outcome is always in doubt.

Robert Nichols

I DROVE ALONG I-20 IN MY HONDA. The dark mass of Atlanta-Fulton County Stadium loomed on my left, the illuminated golden dome of the Georgia State Capitol on my right. I steered the car through a road improvement maze up the exit ramp onto Capitol Avenue, and stopped for a red light by the Capitol.

The passenger-side door of the car opened. A black man stepped into the car, sat down, and closed the door. His entrance was so casual, and the silence afterward so prolonged, I thought at first he had mistaken my car for some other. A fruity smell had come into the car with him.

"Gotta sawed-off shotgun," he said. "Do what I say, or I'll blow your brains out."

"All right."

"When that light change, you drive right on."

"OK."

"Where you going?"

"My wife's waiting for me over there," I said, pointing off toward the university buildings.

"You ain't got no wife!" he barked. The point of the

remark was intimidation. There was an oblique reference to Atlanta's large, predominately white, intown gay population.

"I *do* have a wife," I said—it seemed well to insist on that—"and she's waiting for me over there."

"You ain't got no wife. Keep driving, faggot. I need a hit. Get me money, or I'll blow you away!" He wiggled something in his jacket pocket.

Well, this might be *it*. I had always wondered what *it* was going to be like. Looked as if it might be wall-to-wall reinforced concrete.

"Whatcha got on you?"

"I don't know."

He glanced out the back window to check traffic. "Pull over and stop." I did. He wiggled the thing in his jacket pocket. "Sawed-off shotgun," he said. "Blow you away."

I took the wallet from my pants pocket and held it open for him to see: a one-dollar bill, a practical joke. I recalled those stories of people getting shot in holdups *because* they had nothing to give.

"That it?"

"Yeah."

"Gotta bank machine card?"

I hesitated. "I don't know." What I really meant was, I was not sure I knew how to use the one I had.

"Do you, or don't you? Don't mess with me, faggot white boy!"

"I have a Mastercard," I said.

"Where's it work?"

"Little Five Points, I think." I never used the card to get cash.

"OK, let's go. No monkey-business, hear what I'm

sayin'? I don't want you punching no funny numbers in that machine."

I got back on I-20 headed east. "Should I take the Boulevard exit?"

"No, man, Moreland."

Boulevard would take us to Little Five Points about as directly as Moreland, but not as quickly, probably, and he was in a hurry for that hit.

I drove down I-20 trying to keep the car in its lane, my nervous system under control, and an eye on him. I should be planning something, I thought. But the circumstances were not conducive to the development of schemes.

To gain access to my account at a bank machine, I would have to use a code word, I knew. What was mine? I had a vision of what might happen if I couldn't come up with money once we reached the bank machine.

"This is going to sound like a double-cross," I said, "but I don't think I can get money with my card."

There was a several-second delay while he processed this remark.

"What you mean, you can't get money? You want to get yourself killed, honky?"

I tried to explain my difficulty as succinctly as possible.

"Cut the shit, man, get me the damned money!"

I was getting angry myself. "Look, I'm trying to help. What I'm telling you is, going to Little Five Points will be a waste of time."

My dander quieted him. "Where you get cash?"

"I don't. My wife gets it downtown."

We reached the Moreland exit, and I drove off the freeway.

"Hey, what you doin'? I tell you to turn?"

"You said Moreland, this is Moreland."

He looked around as if not quite sure where he was.

We went up the curved exit ramp onto Moreland. I braked for a red light. "Look," I said, "I know how to get you cash. You know that Kroger store on Moreland?" I pointed south.

"Yeah."

"I can write a check for you there."

"Gotta check on you?"

I usually carried several. I removed my wallet from my pants pocket again, and opened it.

Nothing.

"I'm not far from my house," I said. "I could get a check there."

Should I have said that?

"Where you live?"

"Grant Park."

"Let's go."

Did I really want to do this? Well, I was doing it. I drove south on Moreland to Ormewood, made a right turn, and headed over toward the Park.

"I think there's a fifty-dollar limit for cash at Kroger's," I said. "Will that be enough?"

"Yeah."

Really? I might not get out of this alive, but at least my Mastercard account would be intact.

"Where you live in the Park?"

"Jackson Street."

"Who home?"

"Nobody."

"Better not be.... Don't you go for no gun, neither."

"I don't own one."

On Jackson, we passed the middle-aged black woman my neighbors had dubbed "Wonder Woman," a self-appointed vigilante who roamed our streets at night wearing blue Spandex tops. The heavy object we had speculated was a handgun swagged udder-like in the belt purse at her waist.

I pulled up in front of my bungalow and cut off the car motor.

"My old neighborhood," he said quietly. "Old lady and me lived right up the street there when we first marry."

"At Tyrone's rooming house?"

"Next door.... You know Tyrone?"

"We swap produce from our gardens in the summer."

"Yeah, he always have that garden.... Used to be a Mexican in the basement."

"Chico? He's still around. These days he lives in the shed out back with a German shepherd.... What's your name? Next time I see Tyrone, I'll tell him... "

I laughed at my breach of holdup-victim etiquette. "Well, I guess I'm not supposed to ask that, am I?" I punched him on the shoulder lightly.

He shrank from my touch. "Gotta be a faggot if you live around here. Ain't nobody here but old folks, crazy niggers, and faggots."

"And writers," I said.

"Riders?"

As I got out of my car, Uncle Fester, the pop-eyed, double-chinned, bald Addams Family look-alike strode past, hands clasped behind his back, eyes to the pavement. He was wearing his all-weather black turtleneck sweater.

5

I went up the walk to the house, and onto the porch. I was searching for my door key when my companion realized—none too soon—that it would not be a good thing for me to get into my house alone. He got out of the car and, limping slightly, came hustling up onto the porch.

I turned the key in the lock and pushed the door inward.

Our cat lay stretched out full length on the loveseat in the foyer: Liz Taylor doing Cleopatra. Her eyes went from drowsy slits to green marbles at the sight of the stranger. She arched her back and hissed.

"May have to blow away the damn pussy," my companion said.

I laughed. In the light of the foyer, I saw a hint of a grin flicker at the edge of his mouth. He was a little taller than I. He had regular features and a short beard trimmed recently. His eyes were liquid—he was on something—but they were not unresponsive. There was something in his jacket pocket, all right, and he kept his hand on it.

"There might be cash in the bedroom," I said, recalling the small wicker basket where my wife kept spending money sometimes.

I walked to the bedroom at the back of the house. He followed.

Two or three days worth of socks and underwear festooned the back of a chair. The bed was unmade. A walk-in closet door off its hinges lay horizontally along a wall. A second door I intended to install in place of the other stood vertically against an adjacent wall.

"Excuse the condition of the room," I said, "we weren't expecting company."

Now, he not only knows where we live, I thought, but

where the cash is. But what we saw as I raised the wicker basket lid was not likely to trigger fond memories later in a starved drughead.

"Have to write that check, I guess," I said cheerfully.

A small picture frame containing a snapshot of my wife and her sister stood beside the basket.

"That your wife?" he said.

"The one on the right."

"Pretty," he said—in a way that did *not* disturb me.

"Smart, too. A college professor."

"Thought profs made a lot of money?"

"Depends."

I walked out of the bedroom into the dining room. In the distance, John, our neighborhood drunk, was railing at something or nothing, having polished off his bottle and (as one of our neighbors described this nightly phenomenon) "turned into a pumpkin."

The checkbook lay on the mantel. I picked it up. Behind me, sounds of feet struggling, and then the bedsprings went *scrunch*. My companion must have tripped over something and fallen onto the bed. I tore a check off the pad. "You all right in there?"

He came limping from the bedroom. "Damn house is falling apart."

A wide-brimmed straw hat with an absurd high crown I wore for its shade while revising manuscripts on our side porch lay on the dining room table. My companion paused before it, then put it on his head and approached the small mirror mounted in the mantel to consider the effect.

"Like to have me one of these," he said.

"If you want it, it's yours."

His eyes filled with gratitude. I thought it must have been a very long time since anyone other than chemical demons gave him a gift.

"You know what's wrong with this whole thing?" he said.

"What's that?"

"I'm trying to do my tough guy act, and I'm getting to like you."

"Well, say faggot white boy ten times," I suggested. Had I overstepped a line?

He shook his head back and forth helplessly. "Man, this is unreal."

"*Tell* me about it," I said, slipping into companionable black English. If I had had no clear plan in mind when I brought him home with me, it seemed now that I could not have done better. In his old neighborhood I was not an abstraction. I knew Tyrone and Chico. I had a wife. I did not have much money, obviously. Bringing him home allowed him to imagine that we were of the same ilk.

What he did not know would not hurt him: Only by living where I did, as I did, could I afford my regular writer's hit. I shot up with ink. Paper white I might be, but my soul was really quite black. I was already thinking about my next fix, likely to involve him. I considered offering him a beer.

He seemed less in a hurry for *his* fix now. I did not think he had only needed someone to talk to, but talking had quieted him.

"Need money," he said, "but hate takin' it off a friend."

"What are friends for?"

"You want to go through with this?"

Absolutely, this was getting to be interesting.

We got back into the Honda, drove to Moreland Avenue, and turned south toward Kroger's.

"Used to be a woman at Tyrone's with big titties," he said, "Little slip of a woman, but them big titties."

"Don't think I've ever seen her."

"Big bust," he said nostalgically.

That portion of Moreland Avenue we drove along was a business strip serving a rainbow population of blacks, poor whites, gays, Asians, Latins. There were fast food restaurants, liquor stores, used car and used furniture operations—and Value Village, the Amvets used-everything store.

A sign in front of a used car lot:

> $20,000 BAD CREDIT? NO PROBLEM
> BANKRUPT? NO PROBLEM

What unifies Moreland Avenue, apart from signs on telephone poles for Al's Low-Overhead Plumbing executed, apparently, by Al's own heavy hand, are monsoon-like broken glass rains which sweep over parking lots leaving them sparkling and crunchy.

"Now when we get there," he said, "I don't want you running up to no guard."

"We should buy a few things," I said. "They won't give us cash, otherwise."

We turned off Moreland into Kroger's parking lot.

"Pull right up to the door," he said.

"That's grocery pickup."

"Do what I say, white boy!" He was cranking up the

tough guy act again. "Know what they gonna say in there," he muttered. "Here come the crazy nigger and the faggot white boy." He seemed concerned about his image. I wondered if he remembered he was wearing my hat. I knew about black homophobia, but had never seen it close-up like this. For a guy cruising the streets for highs, doing god-only-knew-what with his sexuality, if any were left, what a magnet for projected emotion the gay! To rip off a gay devil downtown would be a job for Robin Hood—God's work almost.

We entered the store. As if to dissociate himself from me, he led the way. He scooped up three packs of cigarettes from a rack at the rear of the store, then turned around and started for the checkout. Bringing up the rear, I coughed.

"Gotta cold?"

"Sinus problems," I said.

"Getcha some this, clear it right up," he said sweetly, reaching to a shelf and handing me a bottle of Pine-Sol all-purpose cleaner.

I ran a check through a check-approval machine, and we stood in a checkout line behind a few customers.

"I'm going to be writing the check," I said. "Wouldn't it be better if I held the groceries?"

He handed me the cigarettes. "You make everybody feel this stupid?"

"Stupid? What's stupid?"

"Stupid stealing from a *friend*. I ain't robbing you, you giving me a gift."

Robbing someone at gunpoint seemed to be for him a bit like paying a prostitute to be nice.

"You think I gotta gun?" He wiggled the thing in his pocket.

A thickset little black woman in line looked back over her shoulder and up at us with huge brown eyes, dropped a six-pack of Cokes on the checkout conveyor belt, and sprinted for the door. The checkout clerk looked after the woman, then turned to appraise with beady eyes my friend and me. She was one of those super-lean Appalachian white women who would look as if we were in a Depression even if you tied her to a post—or one of her cousins—and force-fed her lard and honey.

"How y'all doing'?" she said, eyes darting back and forth between the faggot white boy and the crazy nigger.

"I'm alive," I said.

I got my man his money, and we left the store. It had been, by my standards, an expensive evening. I assumed that now he had the money, our dealings were concluded. But he opened my car door and seated himself.

"Drop you off somewhere?" I inquired redundantly.

"Freeway," he said.

A fine place, the freeway, for him to drop *me* off. "Are you planning to steal my car?"

"Not now."

The freeway had figured in his original plan. In this instance, as before, he had responded slowly to altered circumstances.

"I'm going up past the Capitol," I said. "I can drop you off there."

"OK."

We got onto I-20 headed west. "You want some of this back?" he said, holding out the fifty dollar bill as if we could slice it down the middle.

"It's yours."

"Mumma would turn over in her grave, if she knew I was messin' round in the street like this.... I come from a good Christian family."

"Me too," I said. "So what are two nice guys like us doing on Moreland Avenue at midnight?"

"Everthin' fucked," he said. "No job, no money.... You gotta job?"

"Not exactly."

"I got two little ones. Old lady and 'em in the projects. I'm gonna take this money, and buy 'em food."

"Good idea."

"You wanna meet my wife?"

The prospect of a guided tour through the projects tempted curiosity strongly. But duty called. "I really have to pick up my wife."

"You can tell your friends tomorrow you run into a crazy nigger downtown."

"You're OK," I said. The other half of the book-title suggested itself: I'm OK.

"I want to pay you back for this loan when I can," he said.

"Well, you know where I live."

"Name William Bailey," he said. "If you don't hear from me, you call me at —- ——." He repeated the phone number twice, slowly, so I would be sure to get it. "You think I gotta gun?"

"I don't know."

He withdrew from his jacket pocket a rolled-up magazine.

"Good bluff."

"I couldn't shoot nobody.... You believe in Jesus?"

"I believe in Jesus," I testified.

We were not only two addicts, and unemployed sons of good women, but brothers in Christ.

The semiphore by the Capitol was red—again. I brought the Honda to a halt. Bailey held out his hand, and what began as a white man's handshake melted into the more intimate black brother fingerlock. "Take it easy, man," he said.

"You too. Good luck."

He got out of the car and shut the door. I reached to the passenger-side door, set the lock, and took several deep breaths as I watched Bailey, still wearing my moonshiner's hat, disappearing into the shadows.

Hester, having put in calls to the Atlanta police, the sheriffs of three counties, the emergency rooms, and the Georgia Bureau of Investigation, was waiting for me in front of her classroom building, as usual.

I recounted my adventure on the way home.

"So you were robbed by the famous Bill Bailey?"

That had not occurred to me, but it was so. "Won't you come home, Bill Bailey?" I sang, "Won't you come home?"

Hester had gone off to bed. It would be some time yet before I was calm enough to sleep, so I sat on the screened porch at the front of the house overlooking our side yard.

On Oak Street, at the foot of the hill below our house, sounds of a basketball being dribbled on pavement, and the scuffle of sneakers. Cars paused briefly near the hoop black teenagers had rigged on a telephone pole as a cover for drug-dealing, then sped off again.

A sudden drenching tropical summer rain drove the basketball players onto Grandma Mitchell's porch at the Oak-Jackson intersection. Through the susurration of rain on trees and shrubs, I could hear the thonk-thonk-thonk of the ball dribbled on the wooden porch floor, and the banter of young men.

The rain had slowed, and the youths dispersed in various directions on foot, when I heard a raspy black woman's voice coming from the dark yard below my porch, "Mr. Author, that you?"

It was New York Doll, an addict-prostitute back in the 'hood recently after an absence of some months. "M'am?"

"I have a new 'Report from the Street' for you.... Can I have some collards from the garden?"

I got out of my chair. "Do you have anything to put them in?"

"No.... And could I have a cold one?"

I went to the kitchen, located a plastic grocery sack for the collard greens, a can of beer, and a flashlight, and went into the yard.

"Where's Hester?" Doll said, as we walked into the vegetable garden at the back of the house.

"She went to bed early."

"Tell her I love these gold shoes she gave me. They fit perfect." She held up one foot. The ballerina-style slipper glowed in the flashlight's beam. She wore bluejeans, a T-shirt, and the standard neighborhood baseball cap which obscured the hairline and made identification of faces more difficult.

She waded into the collard patch. A tiny woman, shapelier before her crack-cocaine habit had thinned her, she would have looked like a ten-year-old boy except for the big hooker's handbag dangling from one shoulder. She picked leaves off the collard plants and dropped them into the grocery sack.

As we walked back to the front of the house, she withdrew from the handbag her newest "Report from the Street," scribbled in pencil on lined school notebook paper, and handed it to me.

"Would you trade me a five-dollar bill for five in coins?" she asked.

"You owe me four dollars, and I'm supposed to trade you five for five?"

"Oh *please*, Mr. Author!"

"Why do you need a five-dollar bill?"

"To get me a place to stay tonight."

"You've got five dollars."

"Mzz Annie don't take coins."

Doll usually spent warm summer nights like that one on the grass behind Abbadabba Wine and Spirits where she met johns. It was more likely her drug supplier who wouldn't take coins. But I opened my wallet and gave her a five, and she handed me in exchange a little bundle of coins fashioned out of a paper towel.

"The guy who gave them to me had them buried, so they're dirty, but they'll clean right up in ammonia."

"Oh boy, just what I wanted to do tonight, clean some coins!"

She giggled. "You're sweet. I gotta get to work." She headed off up the hill on Jackson Street in search of late night opportunities.

In our kitchen, I unwrapped the coins. American coinage

did not hold up as well underground as the buried gold of fable. The coins were not only dirty, but defaced. Some looked as if they might have been pounded by a sledgehammer, or run over by a tank. There was a potato chip-shaped Kennedy half dollar.

REPORT FROM THE STREET
A Bad Experience

This happened last spring. It was a real nice night. Around eight, I decided to walk down Boulevard to see what was happen at the Big H. Soon as I went across the railroad tracks, this gold car (Fifth Avenue) stopped beside me. I had a feeling I knew the guy driving and shouldn't get in. But like a fool I did. "Let's find a place to be alone," he said.

I needed beer and cigarettes first, I told him, so we went up to Chevron for them, and then over to Grant Park. We had two or three beers sitting in the park, and I thought everything was cool. Then he got nervous or confuse. I didn't get what was up.

"Let's move," he said. We drove over to Moreland Avenue. He kept reaching under his seat.

"What are you looking for?" I asked him. I thought he was after a condom. He didn't say anything. He turned into the cemetery. I was beginning to get scare. We just sat there quite a while, without a word. Then he pulled a dagger out from under the seat and dragged me from the car.

"Bitch," he said, "get down on your knees and give me head." He made me give him oral sex *for two or three hours!* All that time, he was running the dagger up and down my spine. I was crying.

"Crying's not going to help," he said.

"I'll do anything you want," I said, "but please don't kill me, I want to see my son graduate."

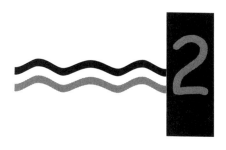

A MILD, SUNNY JUNE MORNING.

At the back of my house, hoe in hand, I intended to weed my garden. But the morning was so fine, I lolled in the garden path watching squirrels play tag through the tall oaks in my neighbors' back lots. Those trees, with early sunlight gilding their leaves, always reminded me of ancient trees in the continental wildernesses painted by early American landscapists.

Apart from the trees and my garden, not much to look at behind the house. An unpaved alley connecting Sycamore and Oak Streets ran along below the garden. On the far side of the alley, a neighbor's backyard featured a rusty supermarket cart tilted jauntily on two wheels, a stack of abandoned truck tires, and a monumental cow-patty (concrete left over from a do-it-yourself project dumped there and hardened into plop art).

I set to work hoeing bean rows.

After a while, long-legged, gangling, crippled Tyrone,

whom Bill Bailey had mentioned, came lurching down the alley with a tall aluminum stepladder balanced awkwardly across his shoulders. The cane that assisted him in walking, ordinarily, dangled from his wrist. The ladder was the kind electricians and stagehands use to get into high places.

"Are you Orville or Wilbur?" I called.

He did not seem to have heard me.

"Got just what you need, man. Nice ladder here, twenty dollars." He always had just what I needed, and I always had just what he needed: cash. The ladder had probably been stolen by an addict who traded it to Tyrone for drugs. Now Tyrone had to unload it cheap and fast in order to buy more drugs for his personal use, or to sell.

"My house has eight-foot ceilings. What would I do with a ladder that tall?"

"Fifteen."

At retail prices, the ladder was probably worth ten times that. "It's not the price…"

"Twelve, my final offer."

I resisted a bit longer, but in the end gave him twelve dollars for the ladder, because I could not endure again hearing the abject pleadings to which he had resorted sometimes on similar occasions. Besides, I had been of a mind lately to throw around money; I had not been myself.

"White woman come down through here?" Tyrone asked, as the two of us lugged the ladder to the crawl space beneath my house.

"I haven't seen anyone."

"Bitch owes me money."

"I ran into a guy you know the other night."

"Later, man," Tyrone said, "gotta get over to the office.

Important business meetin'."

He made his way as swiftly as his damaged spine allowed down the alley and over toward the Oak Street addresses associated with the drug trade. Tyrone had explained his complex gait as the result of a war wound in Vietnam, when I first moved into the neighborhood seven years ago. Later, though, he confessed to having been shot in the back by a cop while fleeing a store he'd burgled.

A smallish white woman I'd never seen before came along the alley the same way Tyrone had been going. She had a mop of bleached-blond hair, and wore a pleated mini-skirt, a red football jersey with a big white numeral 13 on the front, sneakers and sweatsocks. The image was cheerleader. The reappearance of prostitutes following easy money was always a sign that the drug trade, which tended to be gypsy-like in mobility in Atlanta, had swung back our way again.

Attentive to irregularities in the unpaved alley, number 13 picked her way along, and did not notice me until I said, "Easy does it."

Her eyes bringing me into focus had a squirrely intensity.

"I think Tyrone's looking for you," I said.

She looked up and down the alley. "Tell him to stick his head up his ass."

"I'll let you tell him that, if it's OK."

One corner of her thin-lipped mouth rose higher than the other in an ironic smile. "Nice garden. I saw it when I come through here yesterday."

"You live in the neighborhood?"

She fixed me with a look. Was I seeking information that could be used against her?

"I know where to come get my greens," she said.

"Probably enough lettuce here for you, me, and the rabbits."

"I don't like lettuce—but them collards…"

Collards certainly were a hit with the whores lately. But what she was looking at were not collards. "That's broccoli," I said.

She stuck out her tongue. "Ugh!"

The thieves who made off with half my broccoli plants one dark night in May had made the same mistake, I thought. The large dimensions and similar coloration of the two plants probably accounted for the confusion.

No. 13 made her way on down the alley to Oak Street.

When she came back up the alley a few minutes later, I was still leaning on my hoe and woolgathering.

"You're going back and forth, and I'm stationary," I said. "We aren't making much progress."

"Huh?"

"Don't mind me, I'm just babbling." Abstracted many months while finishing writing, I might have struck up conversations that day with trees and possums.

Responsive to my mood, No. 13 came up the garden path. Pointing to her blond hair with one hand, and holding out the other for me to shake, she said, "I'm Sparkle Plenty."

"Yes, you are."

We shook hands. Sparkle held on. She had amazing teeth shooting from her gums at odd angles, forward and backward, side to side.

"Could you loan me five, sir?" she said, gazing into my eyes with burning sincerity. "My little girl needs diapers."

"Loan" in the 'hood was a euphemism. ("Could you loan me a beer?"); the line about diapers was an old standard among area hustlers; and while five dollars *might* be the price of diapers, it was, for sure, what a "nickel bag" of crack-cocaine cost.

"I'd be repaid for this loan?"

"I'd go anywhere with you."

Plaintive and obeisant, rather than aggressively salacious, this appeal went straight from the male eardrum to the bowels, seat of compassion, and ricocheted from there into adjacent parts. What amazing rhetorical subtlety!

"I don't think my wife would approve," I said, "but I can loan you five. I'll have to go up to the house for it, I don't have anything on me."

Going through the back door of my house, I thought, *I never give these people money. Why today?*

"You're of a mind to squander," Georges Bataille explained to me out of the blue. "Parsimony and form secure independence; squandering, a kind of sacrifice, conjures the undifferentiated unity of Being. Long immersed in work in progress, you're more attracted now to chaos than order."

That made perfect sense. Good old Bataille, still batting around in my mind, although I hadn't read his books in years.

I had a five dollar bill in hand as I returned to the garden, but Sparkle Plenty had left. She might have seen Tyrone. Or maybe she thought I was going to call the police?

As I hoed weeds, a phrase from that morning's Atlanta *Constitution* was running through my mind: "an acceptable level of five percent unemployment." In what sense, and for whom, was it "acceptable" that one person in twenty who needed work had none? And the truth was, a lot more people than one in twenty worked at impossibly tedious jobs that paid nothing close to a living wage. The connection between these austere facts of contemporary economic life, and social pathologies bordering on anarchy, was clear enough to anyone living where I did. The previous year, among a population of roughly 400,000 in the city of Atlanta, there had been some 70,000 arrests for drug-dealing, prostitution, armed robbery, house burglaries, and car break-ins and thefts. In a money economy, the "redistribution of the national wealth" wasn't just a radical cause, it was something that *happened*, one way or another.

I had Rolfe Humphries' translations of Juvenal's *Satires* in hand as I stepped out onto my front porch that afternoon. I had purchased the book at the Ohio State University book store in 1959 for $1.25. I knew that, because the price tag was still on the cover. Ever since 1959, I had been intending to read Juvenal's *Satires*. Today was to be the day.

From my porch about halfway up one of Atlanta's countless hills I had a view, uphill and downhill, of bungalows with short front yards. The houses dated from the 1920s and 1930s. Off to my left, Jackson Street descended the hill, crossed Oak Street, and went one block further to terminate at Confederate Avenue. Coming in the other direction uphill at about a forty-five degree angle, Jackson passed my house, intersected with Sycamore, and on the hilltop crossed Boulevard, a four-lane artery running beside Grant Park.

Beep beep!

Somewhere to the south of my house, the day's door-to-door drug deliveries were beginning. Buyers phoned in orders, sellers delivered like pizza men. Horn-honkings announced the arrival of the goods.

Someone started a car parked in front of Grandma Mitchell's house below me at the corner of Oak. Glancing in that direction, I noticed that a fern in Hester's hanging basket arrangement on our porch had disappeared overnight: a modest redistribution of the national wealth. The wide, flat, boatlike 1980s car with faded silver paint pulled away from Grandma Mitchell's and started uphill, bass music blaring from trunk speakers, vibrating metals in the car's loose joints:

*DadadaDOOOOOM . . . .DadadaDOOM-DOOM . . .
DadadaDOOOOOM . . . .Dadadada DOOM-DOOM.*

Grandma Mitchell was operating a bed-and-breakfast for men working in the drug trade, it was said. Running such an establishment in a neighborhood of private residences violated a city ordinance, of course. But this ordinance, like many another expressive of the ruling middle class's desire for peace and quiet, ignored what a lot of people in the inner city had to do in order to survive. Sensibly enough, scarcely anyone in a position to enforce the ordinances took them very seriously. Politicians responsive to the will of a predominately black and poor electorate, and the police who served the politicians, certainly didn't. Enforcing the laws would often have been cruel. Besides, the number of violators made enforcement virtually impossible.

What had attracted my wife and me to the neighborhood when we had come to Atlanta in 1986 was its nearness to the university where she taught, and its modest property values. Realtors at the time had been prophesying a "gentrification" of the area: a euphemism for that process in which middle class people buy up rundown inner-city properties, renovate them, and turn a profit by driving off poor people and their problems. (On the "urban frontier," poor people were the Indians. Our Indians were mainly black, although the number of genuine south-of-the-border Indians had increased steadily.) Under the influence of crack-cocaine introduced into Atlanta's poorer neighborhoods in the late Eighties as "gentrification" was proceeding, the Indians had become increasingly wild.

In the summer of 1991, the sight of gangbanger types in groups of ten and fifteen marching through our decent, if somewhat bedraggled, lower middle-class streets like Hitler's army into Prague was so improbable, that I, like others, had ignored it at first. Surely it would go away. Police at the nearby precinct would not tolerate this for long.

But they had.

The previous summer, things had reached a point at which some of us in the neighborhood had attempted, without much success, to organize a resistance of home-owners. Our neighbors were a hodgepodge of races, classes, ages, educational levels, and points of origin without any natural basis for solidarity; and like contemporary Americans generally, their experience of cooperation for the achievement of civic ends was so small, they were ignorant of its potential force.

Apprised of our situation, City Councilman Lance Albright, one of the mayor's minions, had seemed interested mainly in convincing us that the city's understaffed police force was doing as good a job as could be expected under the circumstances. And maybe he was right.

At the moment our situation was curious, because, depending on where one looked, and when, one saw evidence of gentrification—or an encroaching barbarism. It wasn't at all clear to me which would win out.

Jake Macht was coming down the hill on Jackson in my direction, following his boxer on its leash. A former Green Beret who had spent his late twenties and early thirties in the world's trouble spots, Jake had bought a house up on Boulevard a year ago, only to discover he had come to yet another of the world's trouble spots. His earlier experience of trouble spots having turned him into a chronic insomniac, he would patrol our streets while awake in the middle of the night, his high-tech Glock handgun at his waist. Seeing me on my porch, he crossed the street and came up into my yard.

"On the loose at this hour?" I called to him.

"I'd ask you the same, but I know you're *always* on the loose."

"I detect a note of jealousy."

"Note? It's a brass band!"

"What have you been up to?"

"Just back from a business trip to Chicago. I should be in bed sleeping it off. I *wish* I was doing that."

"The insomnia never lets up?"

"Not really."

Another *beep-beep* somewhere to the south of us. Jake looked in the direction of the sound. "There's a lot of stuff going on in the neighborhood again," he said.

"I know. The effect of the sweeps seems to have worn off."

"What effect was that?"

I smiled.

Drug-selling in the streets had become blatant enough back in early spring to disturb even the most complacent and cowardly of our neighbors. We had organized a call-in to the police precinct in Grant Park. Overwhelmed by calls from homeowners, business people along Boulevard, and real estate agents, the police responded with "sweeps." They set up roadblocks at several points around our area to check auto registrations and driver's licenses. During a sweep, arrests for narcotics possession, usually small quantities, would be made. During one sweep, a drug-dealer executed a tire-squealing U-turn short of a roadblock, and made a run for it. Two patrol cars gave chase and cornered the fellow a few blocks away. Bubba, a drug-sniffing hound of local fame brought to the scene, became highly agitated near one of the car's door panels. When police pried loose the panel, they found a cache of cocaine with a street value of fifty thousand dollars. The excitement in the 'hood that night had been the lead story on Channel Five's late news.

The sweeps with their squad cars, tow trucks, uniformed officers, backed-up traffic, and maybe a television mobile-cam unit or two, were good entertainment for the neighbors who lined curbs to watch. A sweep would create the impression that the police were looking after us. But a month later, men arrested for drug possession, having made the ritual swing through the revolving door of justice at Municipal Court, were back in our midst again (where else?). And we would begin to see the cars that had been impounded, too.

"Where did all these prostitutes come from?" Jake asked. "Tyrone's house is beginning to resemble a bordello."

"They follow the easy money."

"Is Tyrone cooking[1] for the whole neighborhood?"

---

[1]Preparing crack-cocaine from cocaine, baking soda, and water.

"I don't know."

"You and he hang out. I thought maybe you had it from the horse's mouth." Jake smiled at me archly.

"When the horse and I hang out, there are taboo subjects."

"Why does he want to hang with you?"

"Probably to keep an eye on me."

"You find all this interesting, don't you?"

"Yes."

"You are on *our* side?"

I gazed skyward, stroked my chin, and feigned inscrutability. "Kevin's at Tyrone's a lot lately," Jake said. "I thought he was getting out of the drug business after Shit Boy's gang roughed him up in the park."

"Well, that's what he told us, but I think a lot of what he tells us is what he thinks we want to hear. The trouble is, if he doesn't hang with the drug crowd around here, he doesn't have any friends his own age."

"I don't suppose he'll ever finish high school?"

"I doubt it.… Heard about this landscaping business he wants to start?"

"Oh, God yes. I'm constantly getting advice about what I should do with my yard."

I laughed. "Welcome to the club.… He's got a scheme for cutting labor costs in his business: He'll hire only crack addicts and pay them in drugs rather than cash."

Jake shook his head back and forth. "I wouldn't have missed living here for anything."

"I asked Kevin what would happen if some homeowner up in Druid Hills found out drug addicts were tending his lawn. He said, 'If he don't like it, fuck him!'"

"The boy will go far."

"Maggie Spitz is trying to keep him straight. It helps that they have Shit Boy for a common enemy."

"She still chasing him around?"

"She has a warrant for him in the glove compartment of her pickup. That, and a loaded .357 Magnum.... Shit Boy, or someone, pooped on her porch the other night."

"Shit Boy left his calling card."

"Probably."

"How did all that get started?"

"Oh, Shit Boy was hard up for cash one day. He grabbed her kid Jay on his way to a store, and stole a couple bucks off him. She's been on the warpath ever since.... You haven't been patrolling much lately, have you?"

"Not like last summer. I've been out of town on business a lot. It's gotten harder, too. We used to have a couple kids selling nickel and dime bags on a corner last year. Now, they're usually in cars, and there'll be four or five together."

"What should we be doing?"

"You're the elder statesman here, you're supposed to tell me."

"You're the one with officer's candidate training."

"The other night I was thinking, if I had a catapult, I could lob a Molotov cocktail from my backyard onto Tyrone's roof."

"I was hoping for something a little more refined."

"We could accidentally back a concrete truck downhill from Boulevard into the rooming house."

"There's the ever-popular lynching party," I said.

"BYOB," Jake said.

Sid, a neighbor's tomcat, came around the side of my

house. Jake's dog lunged toward Sid, pulling Jake off balance briefly.

"I ran into a couple Englishmen I knew in Europe at a restaurant up in Buckhead the other night," Jake said. "Desmond and Ronnie?" He grinned.

"Cute names."

"Yeah, they're queer, too, but not real cute. They used to be in the French Foreign Legion."

"I thought once you were in the Legion, you couldn't get out again alive?"

"All I know is, they've set up as a gay couple here. I told them about our neighborhood problems. They offered to lend a hand."

"What would they do?"

"Oh, they might close off that section of Oak where the drug boys play basketball, and come in from both ends with ballbats. Crack a few skulls. That kind of thing."

"Could we do that without starting a race war?"

"Can we count on the police to clean up the problem?"

Jake's boxer was straining at its leash.

"Listen, I've got to get this guy on down the road," Jake said, "but let's keep in touch about this stuff. I don't think it's going away any time soon."

"Neither do I."

Watching them descend the hill, I envisioned a pickup vigilante band: Jake, his high-tech Glock handgun at his waist; two graduates of the French Foreign Legion, dish towels hanging down the backs of their necks; Wonder Woman in her blue Spandex; and Maggie with her .357 Magnum trained out the driver's-side window of her pickup.

Glancing down Rolfe Humphries' table of contents, I

noticed Satire Three, "Against the City of Rome." That sounded interesting.

The satire had to do with the decision of the author's friend, Umbricius, to abandon Rome for a rural life.

Umbricius has much on his mind. "Since there's no place in the city,"

He says, "for an honest man, and no reward for his labors,

Since I have less today than yesterday, since by tomorrow

That will have dwindled still more, I have made my decision. I'm going

To the place where, I've heard, Daedalus put off his wings,

While my white hair is still new, my old age in the prime of its straightness,

While my fate spinner still has yarn on her spool, while I'm able

Still to support myself on two good legs, without crutches.

Rome, good-bye! Let the rest stay in the town if they want to.

Fellows like A, B, and C, who make black white at their pleasure,

Finding it easy to grab contracts for rivers and harbors,

Putting up temples, or cleaning out sewers, or hauling off corpses,

Or, if it comes to that, auctioning slaves in the market..."

Sounds downhill brought my eye up from the page. At the intersection of Jackson and Oak, an ample, middle-aged black woman in a baggy yellow sundress and rubber thongs was laboring at some task. As she came up Jackson, I saw that she had two pieces of luggage: a white plastic bag filled with what might be laundry, and a medium-sized pasteboard carton open on top. She toted the plastic bag uphill a few yards and placed it down on the pavement. Then she went back downhill, seized the pasteboard box by one of its cover flaps and tugged it uphill alongside the bag. Then she carried the bag uphill a short distance further, and then the box. Evidently she intended to reach the top of the hill in this laborious way. I glimpsed the contents of the box: billiard balls. I was considering putting an end to her Sisyphean torture by gathering bag, box, and woman into my car and driving them up the hill, when another sight distracted me from that charitable work: Kevin (whose usual summer attire was droopy-drawer shorts, a baseball cap with the bill turned down the back of his neck, and hightop sneakers) came striding down Jackson in a dark blue business suit, long arms swinging chimpanzee-like at his sides.

He crossed my lawn and came to the edge of the porch, where he struck a model's pose, arms extended at his sides. "Howya like my new suit?"

It was an archaic straight-legged job with pin-stripes and narrow lapels suitable for the American businessman, circa 1970. The sleeves of a white dress shirt protruded an eye-catching three or four inches from the jacket cuffs.

"Why all dressed up?"

"Skeeter's funeral."

"Skeeter died?"

He was appalled by my ignorance. "You didn't see it on tv?"

"No."

"Guy shot him in the back down at Englewood."

I stared at him. "A drug deal went bad?"

He nodded in the affirmative. "I was there when it happened."

"Were you selling?"

His eyes shifted out toward the street. "Hanging with the guys"—the guys who would have been selling.

"Pinhead Willis hit him with a shotgun. Hole in Skeeter about like that." He indicated with his thumb and middle finger a diameter of some two inches.

Reaching into his jacket pocket, he extracted a funeral program printed on $8^1/_2 \times 11$ paper folded into quarters, and handed it to me.

HOMEGOING SERVICES
Ramod ("Skeeter") Jeter
Solid Rock Baptist Church
Rev. Daryl Lavell
Officiating

The smiley, thin face in the school photo reproduced crudely on the program's cover was Skeeter's, although without the aid of the program I might not have connected it with the perpetually strained countenance of the young man I'd often seen in the 'hood. There was an acrostic on the inside leaf of the program:

R is for his "readiness," whatever might come.
A is for his "amazing ability."
M is for his "manliness."

O is for his helpfulness to "others" less fortunate.
D is for his "daring."

J is for the "Jello" that he loved. (Smile)
E is for his "extraordinary" talent.
T is for his "tragic" death.
E is for the "everlasting effection" we will have for him.
R is for "remembrance."

— Zoobaka Sherod

Zoo Sherod, author of the acrostic, cruised the neighborhood summer nights peddling crack out of his rusty old brown Nova. The pallbearers listed on the back of the program all worked in the drug trade, too.

My eyes kept returning to Kevin's suit. It was nearly identical to the one I purchased for my father's funeral in 1971, and still had in a closet.

The phone rang in the house. I went inside. The call was a wrong number. Since I was in the house, I went to the bedroom closet where I kept my blue pinstripe suit, and looked inside. It was gone. Never having had anything to sell anyone during my adult life, I had always feared a descent into a poverty in which any clothes I owned would be of value to me, so I rarely disposed of old ones. My wife regarded this retentiveness as compulsive packratting, and in a recent conversation had ridiculed, specifically, my attachment to the blue pinstripe suit I had not worn in twenty-five years. "It's just sitting there mildewing and taking up closet space."

"I might yet need it," I said.

She laughed affectionately. "For a job interview?"

"No, but I could beg in it."

"Wouldn't that be the wrong image for a beggar?"

"I might want to tear a jacket pocket slightly, or cut a hole in a knee. The image of the *lumpen* bourgeois man is very affecting for bourgeois people. You know, 'There, but for the grace of the market…'"

"You don't weigh what you did in the 1970s. You couldn't get into that suit if you wanted to."

"But don't you see, if I had come to the point of needing it, I would have lost enough weight to do so!"

She threw her hands in the air. "One of these days that suit is going to disappear."

A moment's reflection explained how the suit might have made its way from my wardrobe into Kevin's. I suspected Hester had put it in the street for the city sanitation crew on trash pickup day. That day was a weekly treasure hunt for Kevin's mother. A good guess would be that she had come across the suit and taken it home.

I returned to the front porch.

The black woman and her luggage were now pretty far up the hill. Tyrone had shown up in front of my house riding his old balloon-tired Schwinn bicycle, its seat rigged so he could lie back in the saddle like a motorcyclist. In this posture, notwithstanding his disability, he managed to wheel around the neighborhood.

"You have a new backpack," I observed. It was a capacious, shiny blue vinyl number.

"Yeah," Tyrone said. "I carry my tool in it."

"Some tool," I said.

He didn't get the joke. "Going out to pull a job?"

He responded in his aggrieved soprano: "Man, I ain't no burglar! I'm Mr. Fix-It."

"Mr. Fix, more like."

"Now don't do me like that!"

He pointed a long finger at my house roof. "Y'all gotta tree limb hangin' over your house."

"And…?"

"Ah trim it for you cheap."

"You're going to hit me up twice in one day?"

He grinned.

I, too, had noticed that limb—and a squirrel using it as a bridge from my neighbor Wilson's roof to mine several times at sundown. Suspicious sounds in my attic recently suggested the squirrel might have found her way into the house and established a nest.

"What's cheap?" I asked.

"Fifteen dollars."

"You're on."

I had made his day. "Have to be later on, I got things to do today."

He headed off downhill on the Schwinn.

Kevin had been examining the turf of my front yard. Except for the length of the sleeves, my suit fit him reasonably well. The black hightop sneakers were odd accessories.

"That there's Kentucky bluegrass," he said. "Don't see much of that around here. Where'd y'all get that?"

"Came with the house."

He sauntered about the yard, eyes to the turf.

Bill Clinton, the albino cockatoo who summered in his cage on my Wilson's porch next door, screeched, "New York, New York, it's a wonderful town."

"*Caw-caw-caw!*" responded Mzz Grant, an old black woman, from the screened porch of white Mzz Homer's house across the street. The cockatoo answered in kind.

Mzz Grant's voice being naturally shrill, her imitations of the cockatoo were faithful to the original. She and the bird sometimes whiled away summer afternoons calling back and forth.

"Kentucky bluegrass, clover," Kevin said, "Bermuda grass, hens-and-chickens. *D-a-a-a-am!* Y'all gotta little bit of *everything.*"

"I grew up near Marysville, Ohio, home of Scott Seed," I remarked. "You've probably seen the television commercials: 'There's not much to do in Marysville, Ohio, but watch the grass grow.'"

"You *could* have a nice lawn here," Kevin said. "Fix it up. People'd come by and say, 'Look at that, willya?'"

"It would take a lot of work and money."

"You don't get sumpin for nothin," he admonished. "Now what you want to do is spray all this shit with Roundup and let it die off."

His pedagogic voice and manner were not his own. I had the feeling he was parroting someone at the landscaping firm where he had been working part-time.

"Then in the fall, you get you a tiller and start from scratch. If you don't do that, you ain't never gonna have a nice lawn, long as you live."

I imagined one acquaintance of mine saying to another in grave accents at my funeral, "You know, as long as he lived, he never had a really nice lawn"—and a tear moistening the cheek of the latter.

"Spending a lot of time at Tyrone's, are you?" I asked.

He looked out toward the street, and shrugged his shoulders.

"What's new up there?"

"Same ol', same ol'."

"I heard there's a new crowd."

"Buncha geek monsters."

"Geek," the last time I heard anyone use the word, had referred to sideshow alcoholics who swallowed mice and bit heads off garden snakes.

"Geek monsters?"

"Guys what sit around, smoke blow all the time—way you sit around and write."

I might have underestimated the boy.

"Hey, you know that new girl moved in across from Tyrone?"

"The blonde?"

"Yeah…Bubbles."

Last weekend I had seen a young woman with ringlets of honey-blond hair cascading down her back, and a young black man, carrying furniture from a rental truck into a house across from Tyrone's rooming house.

"She's a stripper at a club up in Buckhead," Kevin said. "Know what she told me? I could make two hundred a night dancing at a gay club up there. She said she'd teach me how."

"Would you want to do that?" Kevin the homophobe?

"Shoot, for two hundred a night, I would, long as I don't have to be none."

"We're talking nude dancing?"

"Nah, they wear them fancy jockstraps with sparkles all over 'em."

Someone in the neighborhood turned on a power saw. Kevin, abandoning my company with characteristic abruptness, ran down Jackson to investigate: a junior executive on his lunch break in the Seventies. A sound at his back stopped him. He pivoted to look uphill as couple dozen billiard balls came rolling noisily down the hill, ricocheting off curbs and the tires of parked cars. A black ball hugging the curb as it reached the Oak Street intersection went neatly into a storm drain—Eight ball in the side pocket!

"Da-a-a-a-m!" Kevin said, and continued on his way.

How long had my wizened elderly white neighbor Corinne Boardman been peering at me over the box hedges between our two properties? Nearly deaf, she had obviously not heard the billiard balls coming down the hill. Through the hedge I could see the red fur-lined boots that protected her against cold feet in all seasons.

"Your garden's doing nicely this year," she said, smiling wanly.

"It's all the rain we've had."

"My husband Teddy used to lu-u-u-ve to grow roses! He and Mr. Bottoms—the Bottoms lived where you do now— he was so nice—so was Mzz Bottoms. Bouncy they called her. She would do anything for you. They're down in Riverdale now. Of course, I haven't seen them in years. She's not getting on very well, I hear. They found out she had leukemia right after they moved down there."

Mzz Boardman paused at this point in the Bottoms monologue, as she had every time I had heard it, to shake her head back and forth at the shame of Mzz Bottoms' illness which, however, did lend support to her belief that venturing out of our neighborhood invited encounters with monsters of Terra Incognita. She had personal experience of this, having in 1939 eloped to Chicago with a fellow who turned out to be an alcoholic wife-beater and philanderer. Her father and an uncle had to take the train north to rescue her. Back home, she had married a young man from the neighborhood, a policeman, and never again left Grant Park. She didn't think anyone else should, either. The detail from her Chicago misadventure that seemed to have impressed her indelibly—she had mentioned it to me a dozen times—was the fact that garbage can lids in Chicago froze tight in January.

Once Mzz Boardman set one of her standard monologues in motion, she felt obliged to let it run all the way to the end. The only way to prevent this from happening, I had learned through harsh experience, was to turn my attention elsewhere. Juvenal was at hand, so I turned my attention to him, and kept my eyes on the page until I heard Mzz Boardman shuffling along the side yard toward the back of her house talking to herself.

3

TYRONE AT MY DOOR. Did I want my tree trimmed today?

"Sure."

"Two man job. Need your help."

"OK."

"Gotta handsaw and some rope?"

"I don't have rope, and my saw's too dull for that."

"Go ahead set up your ladder, I'll be right back."

I was about to go in quest of my extension ladder when I noticed through front windows of my house a late-model Cadillac with gold wheel rims parked in front of a house uphill across the street. I picked up the binoculars I kept near to hand and trained them on the California license tag at the back of the car, but couldn't read it.

Two Hispanic men I had never seen before came from the house. I had positioned myself deeply enough in the dark room to be invisible, I thought. But my impression was that the men were looking my way as they got back into the Cadillac. They drove off.

Three young black men in their twenties or early thirties had recently rented that house, 533 Jackson. None worked regular hours, but all drove new cars and dressed fashionably. There were lavish weekend parties with lots of flashy women. A band of black teenagers dressed identically in fresh white T-shirts, tails outside the pants, showed up periodically at the house.

I settled the aluminum extension ladder against the oak tree Tyrone was to trim. "Have a nice day," croaked Clinton the cockatoo from his cage on Wilson's porch a few yards away.

I leaned against the ladder, awaiting Tyrone's return. My 1979 Toyota had been standing there in my side yard ever since it broke down in late winter. It was not getting any lovelier. While not working, I must arrange for its disposal.

Tyrone came reeling downhill on foot, his cane tapping the pavement. He had a bow saw in hand, a loop of clothesline rope over one shoulder.

I steadied the ladder for him as he made he way up into the tree. Only a few stitches in his trousers' crotch seam were intact. White underwear showed between them.

"Used to trim trees for the Board of Education," he said.

"You never told me that."

"Lotta stuff I don't tell you."

"Probably just as well."

He managed to find a comfortable position straddling the limb he was to cut.

"Is trimming trees dangerous work?" I asked.

"Can be. Limbs don't always fall the way you expect."

I contemplated the narrow space into which the lopped limb would have to fall between the defunct Toyota at the side of my house, and Wilson's new wooden fence. "Will this one?" I asked.

A show of teeth from on high. "Oh, yeah!"

Dumbo, a fat, unshaven white youth in his early twenties who had "not been right" (as his mother put it) since being hit by a car up on Sycamore years ago, walked past my house en route to the trampoline in Maggie Spitz's backyard where he played with neighborhood children.

A swirled mass of cloud in an otherwise blue sky overhead reminded me of a coiled snake.

Tyrone was struggling to notch the underside of the limb he was to cut with the bow saw when Kevin came loping down Jackson, long arms swinging. He was back in his usual garb: floppy shorts, a baseball cap on backward, black hightop sneakers.

"Here comes advice," I said to Tyrone, who looked up from his work and out to the street.

"I know *that's* right."

Kevin, having seen us, left the sidewalk and crossed my lawn. "Whatcha all doin'?"

I told him.

Kevin informed us of the necessity of using a guide rope while trimming a tree, and explained how best to attach the guide rope to the limb.

Tyrone and I exchanged a look. "I'd never have figured that out in a hundred years," I said.

"Me neither," Tyrone said.

Aware of being put on, but not sure why, Kevin chose

this moment to announce that he hoped, once he started his own landscaping business, to hire me as his staff hedge-trimmer. He had observed my competence in this specialty.

"What's the pay?"

"More than you makin' now."

"Like what?"

"Nine dollars an hour, if you work hard."

"I'm a writer, Kevin."

His small eyes brimmed with sarcasm. "Bet you don't make no nine dollars.... Need a rock." He went down along Wilson's fence looking for one.

I described to Tyrone my recent adventure with Bill Bailey, who had said he knew Tyrone.

"You lucky to be alive, man. Some of them niggers downtown is crazy."

Tyrone couldn't remember anyone named Bailey having lived on Jackson. But the turnover of population in the rental houses and rooming houses in the area was constant, and a lot of people had aliases. He thought he might recognize Bailey, if he saw him.

"This ought to work," Kevin said, looking at the long, narrow rock he had found along the fence.

"Kevin and I were discussing boa constrictors the other day," I said to Tyrone. "He claimed they could swallow a human being. I said I didn't think so. Do you know?"

"Yeah, they can," Tyrone said. "They stretch 'emselves real big and gulp you down."

"See, I told you," Kevin said.

I envisioned a stereotypical Englishman in Africa—safari-shorts, pith helmet, pince-nez—disappearing headfirst into a boa constrictor.

"I suppose the snake would lie around about six months afterward digesting," I said.

"Yeah," Tyrone said. "Spit out a bone now and then."

"Burp," I said.

Kevin liked "burp."

"Well, let's get crackin' here," Tyrone said. "Gotta lot to do today."

"Gotta get his crack fast," Kevin translated.

Addicts in the hood, not always skilled at odd jobs, were invariably swift.

"You know why they call Georgia people 'crackers,' Kevin?"

"They all smoke crack."

"No. The early Georgia farmers had teams of oxen. The whips they used made a cracking sound."

"Used them on black folks, too," Tyrone said from on high.

Kevin tied one end of the clothesline rope around the stone he had found, and flung this little package over the limb Tyrone would be cutting. Removing the stone from the rope, he tied a slipknot and pulled it tight against the limb.

"Professional," Tyrone said.

"Very," I agreed.

Tyrone began to cut the limb with long, even strokes of the saw.

"Somebody stole one of our ferns the other night," I told Kevin.

He looked toward the front porch of our house. "They sure did...I seen Shark with a fern up to Tyrone's...Hey, Tyrone, you see Shark with that fern last night?"

"Nah."

at could a person buy with a fern?" I asked.

aybe half a hit," Kevin said.

An old compact car with a bad muffler and faded green paint came rattling past my house. Kevin bolted for the street like a cat in which a hormone had dropped, to stand on the curb gazing uphill. Then he ran down Jackson to Oak Street.

"What's that all about?" Tyrone asked.

"I don't know."

The cloud overhead really did look like a coiled snake, or serpent. I tried to looked skyward at least once a day to remind myself that what lay overhead was not the painted dome of my house, or the backdrop for my act. These things seemed harder to remember than one would expect, given the facts of the case. What made the steady awareness of them impossible were the duties and exigencies of everyday life. As long as you kept your nose to the grindstone, the universe seemed to gravitate around the grinder. That was how it was, and how evidently it was supposed to be. All well and good for the Buddhist monk in his cave or monastery, or wandering like a cloud, to tell us to be mindful of the illusoriness of things. But for people doing the world's work (and filling the monk's begging bowl) that was impossible. Our absurd exaggeration of the importance of our endeavors was written into the necessity of their performance. The tree did not fall in the forest if no one were present to hear it; and infinite space did not exist while people under the sky-dome were doing what needed to be done.

Blaise Pascal had mentioned in his *Pensées* being terrified by the thought of infinite space. But it seemed to me an important omission that he did not say how frequently or prolongedly he experienced this terror. Pascal, in addition to being a busy man of the world, had other *penseés* unrelated to the terror of infinite space. Was he thinking about infinite space while having these other thoughts? How would that have been possible? If infinite space really were terrifying, one would expect it to be so a bit more consistently.

There must be some connection between the general obliviousness of humanity to infinite space generated by the necessities of ordinary life, and the fact that otherwise commonsensical people so generally embraced the extraordinary idea of a life after death. As long as one was going sensibly about his or her daily chores, one felt immortal. The work of the world was not performed by mortals, but by gods.

Somewhere in the distance: *Dadada DOOOOOM! da-doom…Dadada DOOOOOM! da-doom.*

Kevin came back uphill accompanied by Maggie Spitz and her twelve year-old daughter, Angie.

"You guys see Shit Boy go past?" Maggie said.

"I did," Kevin said.

"Well, I know you did, Yellow Dog. You just came and told me that! I'm asking these guys."

Dimple-cheeked Kevin grinned: What, me worry?

Angie's attention fixed on Kevin made me understand in a way I never had before the term "crush." Her eyes were like small blue berries squeezed in a press, emitting sweet juices.

"I was on the phone talking to Sergeant Walker at the precinct about what Shark done, and Shit Boy came right past the window and leered at me!"

"Showing you he ain't scared," Kevin said.

"What did Shark do?" I asked.

"Oh, Chad and I had this old fridge we wanted to get rid

of? Still worked, more or less. You know, mushy ice cream. I figured Shark could make a few bucks on it, so I gave it to him, and loaned him our pushcart to haul it out of the house. What's he do? Takes the damn fridge and the cart over the pawnshop in Lakewood and gets ten bucks for each!"

"Dumb muthafuk," Kevin said.

"How'd you find out about it?"

"He was bragging to John."

"John the Drunk, or John the Dope."

"John the Drunk…I gotta warrant out for the bastard."

"You gonna have a warrant out for the whole 'hood before long," Tyrone said.

"Yeah, honey. While I'm at it, I'm gonna bust your crooked ass, too."

"Crooked, but still works. Wanta give him a try?"

"Aw, go cut your limb, Tyrone. While you're at it, whack off sumpin else!"

"I'd miss ol' blackjack."

"No one else would."

"I ain't so sure about that."

"You men never are."

Maggie, Tyrone, and I were laughing.

Angie snuck up behind Kevin, reached around his waist, and tickled him vigorously.

"Damn it, Angie, stop it!" he complained.

"Angie!" Maggie said.

"How's it going?" I called up to Tyrone.

"Gonna take a while," he said. "This saw seen its better day."

An automatic weapon—*bam-bam-bam-bam-bam*—fired

somewhere in the vicinity of the Atlanta Federal Penitentiary to our south.

Maggie and I wandered into my backyard to examine the progress of my garden. "That's a half-assed broccoli patch you got!" Maggie said, laughing.

I described the great broccoli heist of early May.

"Guys from the rooming house?"

"Probably."

"They spend all their welfare money on drugs, then have to come up with food."

"Hester wanted me to ask you how well you know Uncle Fester."

"Fester? I've lived next door to him two years. Why?"

"Oh, he's been following her down to the bus stop on Confederate every morning and trying to strike up conversations."

"He's probably got a thing for her. Tell Hester not to be too flattered. He's got a thing for just about anything in skirts…Sometimes he puts on bikini briefs and struts around in front of their kitchen window tryin' to get me all hot."

"Fester in bikini briefs? This I would like to see!"

"No you wouldn't, it's enough to make a person throw up."

"He really does look like that guy in the Addams family."

"Oh hell yes!…Tell Hester, he's just a dirty old man… Who're these new guys up the street at 533?"

"We're trying to figure it out."

"I see them in the park weekends cruising around on seven and eight hundred dollar bicycles."

"Are they dealing over there?"

"Probably, but I ain't seen it."

"Are there a lot of drugs in the park on the weekend?"

"Honey, you can get just about anything your little heart desires.... Hey, you know what I just found out? My husband was in a motorcycle gang back in the Seventies."

"Chad? He's so laid-back."

"Yeah. We've only been together three years, and he's quite a bit older than me. I'm still finding out things about him. Some of his old buddies were at the house Saturday night. They had a picture of him on his hog. Used to have hair all the way down to his ass. They called him Moses."

"Chad?"

"I told his friends what Shit Boy done to Jay. They went up to the Chevron station and beat shit out of some guys dealin' over by the public phones."

"Chevron? I thought Shit Boy and his gang worked up near Amoco."

"They do. I told the guys they'd find him at the gas station on Boulevard, but forgot about there being two. They went to the wrong one. Guys was dealin' there, too, so..."

There's a way to get a race war started, I thought.

"Gettin' close!" Tyrone called to us. Maggie and I went back to the tree. I picked up the guide rope and pulled it taut. Tyrone put his back into the work.

CRACK!

"Timmmmmmmmm-ber!" Kevin bellowed.

I guided the cut limb down into the space between the old car and Wilson's fence.

"Caw-caw-caw!" exclaimed Bill Clinton.

"Caw-caw-caw!" replied Mzz Grant from Mzz Homer's porch across the street.

"Congratulations!" I called to Tyrone. "Kevin couldn't

have done that any better."

Tyrone dropped the bowsaw to the ground. "I wouldn't go that far."

Maggie and I steadied the ladder for him. Turning himself around in the crotch of the tree in preparation for his descent, Tyrone presented his backside to us.

Maggie giggled. "Hey, Tyrone, what happened to your pants?"

"My pants?" Craning his neck over his shoulder to look at his rear end, Tyrone nearly lost his footing in the tree.

I opened my wallet and gave Tyrone a five and a ten, and handed Kevin a five. Squandering money was fun, once a century.

Tyrone eyed Kevin's five. "What's he get paid for?"

"Consultant's fee," I explained, winking.

"For twenty, I could give you advice *and* trim the tree."

Tyrone searched in the weedy growth along the fence for the bow saw he had dropped, but could not find it. Neither could the rest of us when we looked.

"Well, it didn't fly away," Tyrone said. "I'll find it later."

My three neighbors were walking down the hill together, as Wilson, a high school teacher on summer break, arrived home in his car.

"My skylight was leaking last night in the rain," Wilson said, coming up the walk to his house. "Do you have a stepladder that will reach twelve feet? I loaned mine to a friend."

"As a matter of fact, I do—as of this week."

As we walked to the back of my house. I explained how I had come by the ladder. Wilson rolled his eyes. We toted the ladder onto his front porch.

"New York, New York, it's a wonderful town," screeched Clinton.

"Good afternoon, Mr. President," I said.

"Blue skies are smiling at me," Clinton said.

That evening at sunset, I sat on the screened porch at the side of our house which faced the oak Tyrone had trimmed.

A squirrel—the one I thought was nesting in our attic—came from the far side of Wilson's roof over the ridgepole, down the near side, leapt nimbly from the roof into the oak, and scurried up the trunk eight or ten feet. There she froze, perplexed by the disappearance of the bridge to my roof. She returned to Wilson's roof, scampered up to the ridgepole, and down the far side of the roof, invisible to me now. But a few minutes later, she peered over the ridgepole at the tree, as if to verify she had not been mistaken.

Where did a squirrel without its nest spend the night?

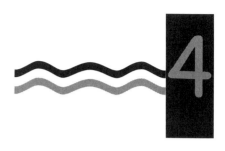

I WALKED IN GRANT PARK. The sky overhead was not the dome of my house or the backdrop of my act. But I was thinking of my Ohio father, with the sky as the dome of his house and the backdrop of his act, who made an excellent living, and did a fair amount of good in the world. Only in the last months of his life, after a series of heart attacks, had he purchased an expensive portable telescope he lay beneath for hours at a time in his back yard, scanning the heavens. Lord only knows what he hoped to see.

I had no doubt taken up sky-watching prematurely, but once one started, there was no way back. You either take this world seriously, or you don't. How, though, did so many succeed in keeping a straight face? Vice-President Gore had recently proposed installing a camera on a satellite that would provide Internet-users a constant live image of the earth in space, to remind them of the unity of humanity on this small planet. But it didn't seem to me that would necessarily be the message people would take from that image.

I was returning home from my walk when I passed the

house below mine on Jackson formerly owned by the Kitchens family that Tamara Thompson, a black woman with a teenage daughter, had bought. Denetia Green, who sold real estate around the Park, had introduced me to Tamara one day back in the spring when the house was changing hands.

Today, Tamara was on her porch looking through her mail, and waved to me. "Excuse our mess," she said, pointing to the mound of rotten lumber, decayed window frames, and dismantled plumbing pipe at the curb in front of her house.

"Don't worry about it. Most of us around here have been through the tear-it-out stage."

We chatted about rising property values in the neighborhood, and I broached delicately the subject of drug-dealing.

"Oh, I'm sure it's around," Tamara said. "I haven't noticed it."

Close to the drug scene on Oak Street as she was, how could she not have noticed it?

"There isn't anywhere in Atlanta you won't find drug-dealing," Tamara said. "The lady across the street told me about Mrs. Kitchens' son."

The previous winter, after a drug deal went bad, two black teenagers invaded the Kitchens' house (now Tamara's) and shot Delbert Kitchens, a pear-shaped white teenager, in the buttocks. Delbert fled the house screaming, clutching the affected portion of his anatomy as if it might fall off. The Kitchens had put their house up for sale the next day.

"We have a network of neighbors who keep in touch about the situation by phone," I said. "You're welcome to join the group, if you like."

"Let me get your number," she said. She invited me into her foyer. There, her daughter's school bag hung from a hall tree. Reaching into the bag, Tamara came out with a pair of index cards and a yellow pencil. We jotted our names and phone numbers on the cards, and exchanged cards. Hers read "Tamika Thomas."

I remembered Denetia Green having introduced her as "Tamara," because I had thought at the time, a Biblical name. And hadn't the last name Denetia mentioned been "Thompson" or "Thomson," not "Thomas"?

When I reached home, Jake Macht and his boxer were examining a terra cotta-colored fire ant mound a half a foot high in my front yard, at the edge of the pavement. The boxer was trying to stick his nose in it.

"That's one of the more impressive anthills I've seen around here this summer," Jake said.

"It used to be up that way," I said, pointing toward the high end of my lot. "I ran the mower over it, so they rebuilt it down here."

"You don't get rid of fire ants, you just move them from one place to another."

"Like drug-dealers."

In a fit of experimental cruelty, I had driven the mower over the mound, lopping several inches off the top and sending a cloud of orange clay dust into the air. Hundreds of pinholes opened simultaneously all over the anthill as the denizens fled the devastation. There had been a considerable increase in the number of explorer ants in our house ever since. You mess with our house, and we'll mess with yours?

A commercial van with "Southeastern Cable" painted on

its side drew up in front of Mzz Homer's house across the street. The driver, a black man, turned off the motor and sat behind the wheel making notes on a clipboard.

"Is what's-her-face still our second-shift beat cop?" Jake asked.

"Atalanta Timmons? Yes, as far as I know."

"Do you ever see her patrolling?"

"No."

"Neither do I. Why is that?"

"Her beat takes in something like four to six square miles. Investigating a traffic accident or a domestic dispute will probably take an hour..."

"So she's never patrolling?"

"Not likely."

"Good-looking woman."

"Yeah, she was Miss Black Atlanta one year, as a teenager. Rumor has it she also made a couple softcore skinflicks."

"So how'd she get to be a cop?"

"The story I heard is, she had a rebirth experience, and went straight from that to the police academy."

Jake guffawed.

Boing, boing, boing, boing, boing.

Shark Cryder, the only person I ever knew who could make cheap false teeth twang like a jawharp, was coming down the hill toward us.

"Hey, man!" he called to me from across the street. "Tyrone says y'all think I stole your fern."

"Somebody took it, I don't know who."

"Tom Payne had a fern. Ask him about it."

"Yeah, I will."

Shark went on down the hill.

"Melinda Spack had some plants stolen from her porch, too," Jake said.

The workman got out of the van, removed a ladder from a rack, and set it up against a telephone pole in front of Mzz Homer's house.

"Kevin was asking a lot of questions about the police sweeps the other day," Jake said. "He seemed to be trying to find out who was responsible."

"He's done that with me, too. The drug boys probably want to know."

"Haven't they got anything better to do with their time?"

"I doubt it. If all you have to work with is a molehill, you make a mountain of it." It occurred to me that I had just described succinctly my aesthetic, diet, political life, wardrobe, entertainment, and stock market investments.

"A guy in law enforcement I know says we're attracting gangs chased out of Southern California." Jake said. "If there's only one beat cop for every six square miles, you can kind of see why."

A public address speaker mounted on the workman's van began broadcasting a radio sermon by a black preacher.

"Now, you see these pretty little ladies going down the street with their short little skirts and their bare legs, and those cute little packages of theirs a-twitchin'. [Muffled laughter from the congregation.] You see girls walkin' on Peachtree Street wearin' bras!"

"I know *that's* right," said a woman's voice.

"I dreamed I walked down Peachtree Street in my Maidenform—but it ain't no dream!" [Laughter]

"And you see young bucks with their eyeballs poppin'

out of their heads, too—and can you blame em?"

"You tell it like it is!"

"Now, we all know how children get born. It ain't that hard a thing to do!...But the question is, do these folks what knows how to get children know what to do with them once they get born?"

"Amen."

Jake, the boxer, and I retreated from the street to my porch, distancing ourselves a bit further from the sermon.

"So what do you tell Kevin about the sweeps?" Jake asked.

"I tell him I think the people up on Lee Street probably organized them."

Jake grinned. "Brilliant idea. Why didn't I think of that?"

When we had been organizing the mass call-in to the local precinct in March that led to the sweeps, we had tried with little success to enlist the help of residents along Lee Street. Their houses were more elegant than ours. Their reluctance to join forces with us had seemed to me, in part, snobbery.

"What's wrong with those people up there, anyway?" Jake asked.

"They haven't taken direct hits the way we have."

"Yeah, but they're only a block from where people are taking direct hits."

I was sitting quietly on my porch doing nothing, when Wilson called to me from next door.

"You know what? Somebody stole that ladder you

loaned me from my crawl space. I'm going to have to buy you a replacement."

"That won't be necessary, Wilson. I wouldn't have had much use for it. I told you how I came by it... Think of it as our contribution to the redistribution of the national wealth."

Wilson's eyebrows went up.

A UPS truck pulled up in front of Mzz Homer's bungalow across the street. The driver honked his horn once and dashed to Mrs. Homer's door with a package in hand. He was the muscular, lean young Hispanic angel who often delivered gadgets and nostrums the widows ordered from mail order catalogues they had shown me: a talking watch, Ginkgo Biloba ("helps increase blood circulation to the brain"), a ball-point pen look-alike called the Pain-Zapper filled with "special crystals to stimulate nerves at the pain site."

"Who's there?" Mzz Homer cried nasally from somewhere inside her house.

Mzz Grant opened the door of the screened porch. "Why, it's my boyfriend!"

As leery of the conversational quicksand at that address as I was, the UPS guy was leaning back toward his truck even as he handed Mzz Grant the parcel. He hopped back into the driver's seat, tooted goodbye, and off he went.

"Well, see you in the next world!" Mzz Grant shouted to the back of the truck: her standard response to hasty departures from her presence.

She shook lightly the parcel. I suspected it contained the "Bionic Ear" the women had told me they were ordering from a mail order house in Minnesota. The catalogue advertisement claimed that the ear could "zoom in on a whisper at a hundred yards." It promised to enhance their already detailed surveillance of neighborhood life.

Noticing me on my porch, Mzz Grant called across the street, "How you feeling today?"

"I'll do."

She cackled. "You'll do?...Lordy, lordy, sometimes I don't know who crazier, you or me...Whatcha up to?"

"Not much. You?"

"Sold a lotta candy today."

"Good!"

She and her friend Mrs. Homer had been running a candy store on the latter's porch that summer, charging neighborhood children for sweets exactly what Mzz Homer's daughter Sue had paid for them at a wholesaler's. Kids came from blocks away to buy the candy. That, of course, was the whole idea of the thing.

"Caw-caw-caw!" screeched Bill Clinton from Wilson's porch.

"Caw-caw-caw!" screeched Mzz Grant. "Hey, baby, come down to the street, I want to show you sumpin."

She pointed out to me a big, wiggly cross someone had etched with a sharp object in the sidewalk concrete.

"Shit Boy was out here in the middle of the night puttin' a whammy on y'all."

"Hoodoo?"

"Uh-huh."

"What's he got against us?"

"Maybe because you friends with Mzz Maggie."

Yes, that might explain it. Or my involvement with the police sweeps that someone could have leaked. Or my acquaintance with Jake Macht, well-known for his night patrols.

"He done this cross first," Mzz Grant said, "and then he scattered conjure dust over there so you be sure to walk in it."

"What's conjure dust?

"Different stuff. Red pepper, salt, graveyard dirt... If you walk in it, brings bad luck."

"You believe in hoodoo?"

"Some folks does. What you want to do is sweep your walk real good. You see black folks sweepin' all the time, they think somebody layin' a spell."

When in Rome...I went into the house for our corn broom. Mzz Grant looked on with approval as I swept my walk.

"You know they had the wake for Junior down to Grandma Mitchell's house Sunday?" she asked.

"Yes." From our back yard, I had seen the party in progress downhill. The earthy pungency of marijuana smoke had filled the 'hood. There had been long tables filled with food and drink, and a blaring stereo. Mike, one of Tyrone's roomers, had told me that John the Drunk got into a fight at the wake and someone broke his nose—again.

Junior, an addict and petty thief, had stayed at his grandmother's house on and off for years, when not in jail. While he was around the 'hood, if anyone missed anything of value, the police had routinely picked Junior up for questioning. The rumor was, he had died of AIDS. Toward the end of his life, he had had the gaunt look of the victims of that disease.

"When they had him laid out down there," Mzz Grant

said, "the police knock the doe and they say, 'Where Junior?' Grandma say, 'What y'all want with him?' They say, 'We got a warrant for his arrest.' Grandma, she say, 'Well, you welcome to him, officer, but I don't know if y'all wants him in your jail.'"

A gun, or backfiring car, popped like a rimshot somewhere nearby.

"Early target practice today?" I said.

"Them drug boys get on my nerves sumpin awful!" Mzz Grant said. "Be a drug boy, you gotta have a big old gun and a big old car."

"Did Junior die of AIDS?" I asked.

Mrs. Grant nodded yes.

"Was he using dirty needles?"

She looked around to see who might hear what she was about to reveal. "Junior was a morphadite," she whispered.

"A what?"

"Morphadite—half-man, half-woman." She rolled her eyes. "What the world comin' to? . . . Hey! I got some cans for y'all. Let me go up to my house and get 'em, for I forget."

She started up the hill toward her little shotgun house on Sycamore.

Mzz Grant and I had an arrangement: If I was not busy, I drove her to the post office for her welfare checks, the supermarket, the drugstore, the carryout window at Captain D's Fish and Chips, the free clinic for "dates" with her "cute" psychologist. (She had been seeing a psychologist ever since she attacked with a ballpreen hammer the late Mr. Grant, who was asleep at the time. That had been years ago. Grant, surviving the attack, had gone on to perish of natural causes.

"I just about drove that poor man crazy," Mzz Grant had once admitted to me.)

In return for my chauffeuring, she deposited on my porch several times weekly her fuchsia plastic laundry basket filled with aluminum beer and soda cans she had dug out of neighbors' trash. I would transfer the cans into plastic lawn bags. To help support my writing habit, and for something to do when I was at loose ends, I would toss the bags into the back of my Honda, and drive them to the aluminum recycling plant near the penitentiary. A carload of cans would bring ten or fifteen dollars in cash.

Mzz Grant came stumping down the hill, the aluminum can-filled laundry basket pressed to her belly.

Tyrone, coasting downhill on his Schwinn, passed her without a word and turned the bike onto the sidewalk in front of my house. He dropped his feet to the ground.

"Well, if it ain't Mr. Crips the gangster man," Mzz Grant shot at his back.

Tyrone glanced over his shoulder. "Here comes ol' Nosey the welfare queen."

"Cans for you, baby, not the nigger," Mzz Grant said, coming across the lawn to my porch.

"Ain't no problem with that," Tyrone said. "Cans enough for everybody."

A black man driving a wide, low, rust-covered 1980s car of the type Kevin called a "dudemobile" honked his horn as he passed by. Tyrone managed to get his damaged torso cranked around on the bike seat to wave belatedly at the back of the car.

"There's something I don't get," I said to Tyrone. "You're the guys who like car horns. Why are we the honkies?"

"Gonna tell my friends that one," Tyrone said. "Hey—drive me over to the recycling plant. I got some cans... I pay you."

"Would we be making drug deliveries along the way?"

"Ain't gonna do that."

"I'll take you down there."

"I'll go get my shit together. Meet you up to the house."

Innocent of the local scene shortly after I moved into it, I would drive Tyrone, and maybe a crony or two, around the park on "errands." We would stop in front of a house. Tyrone would toot my horn several times, then go inside, returning to the car a few minutes later. We might make three or four such stops in an afternoon. Eventually I realized I was assisting in the distribution of drugs.

I was on my front porch emptying into plastic trash bags the cans Mzz Grant had brought me when the phone in the house rang.

Hester on the line from her office: "This is going to be ten-cheese lasagna night," she said. "I put it out to thaw."

"Yeah, I noticed it on the kitchen counter," I said. "It weighs a ton."

The ten-cheese lasagna was a gift of our neighbor Katie, whose elderly father manufactured the stuff in his kitchen down on Confederate Avenue.

I told Hester about Shit Boy's hoodoo on our front walk.

"That makes me furious!"

I got into the Honda and drove up Jackson to Tyrone's rooming house.

A pile of black plastic yard bags filled with aluminum cans was at the curb. Beside the bags stood Tyrone and a blubbery, puffy-faced white youth with a bad complexion and a gut hung in the sling of a dirty white T-shirt.

A small, slender black woman with paradoxically huge breasts overflowing a halter top stood on the rooming house steps talking into a cellphone.

I got out of my car. Tyrone introduced me to Billy, a new resident at the rooming house. I shook hands with a jellyfish.

"He's OK," Tyrone said to me confidentially.

The woman with the big bust looked at me suspiciously. "I don't think he's talking about me," she said into the phone. "Have to wait and see."

I opened the hatchback of the Honda. Tyrone put his cans into the back of the car. "Could we make a stop in Lakewood?" he asked.

"What for?"

"Billy wants to go to the pawnshop."

"Why?"

"He got sumpin to sell."

"What?"

Tyrone hesitated visibly, but then rolled out from behind a thick pine tree in the yard a used garden tiller. Lawn and garden equipment stolen by addicts, fenced by dealers, often wound up in pawnshops.

"There's no room for that with the cans," I said.

"Make two trips."

"No."

Tyrone and I set off for the recycling center, sans Billy.

"You ain't writin' these days," Tyrone said.

"No, giving it a rest."

"Ain't seen you wearin' that hat of yours." He did an imitation of shoulders-hunched me on my porch leaning over a manuscript.

"Make a million dollars if you wrote up my life story," he said.

Remarkable, how many of my neighbors had expressed to me their conviction that the world was just dying to hear their scintillating personal histories. But that is how his or her life seems always to a person with a sky-dome overhead.

"You'd want a cut," I said.

"Just ten percent!"

"Well, let's see—ten for you, fifteen for my agent Lawrence Lucre…That's $250,000 right there. That would leave only three-quarters of a million. The IRS would want most of that…Not really worth the trouble, when you think of it."

"Tss, tss, tss, tss, tsss, tss, tss."

We passed a wonderfully shapely, long-legged young black woman on a bicycle. She wore short-shorts. The red tongue of the bike seat protruded from between her thighs. Tyrone was struggling to get the passenger's-side window cranked down with his right hand, while fumbling with his left for my car horn .

Beep beep beep beep.

He craned his neck out the car window. "Mama, you sho do look fahn!"

Mah sentiments exactly. The woman had lowered her eyes, but was smiling, I noticed in the car's rearview mirror. Tyrone, observing the direction of my attention, said, "That's Lala."

"I'll say."

"She's around the hood ever now and then. I introduce you sometime, if you ain't writin'."

"Yeah, I know you, Tyrone. You'd introduce me to Lala, then blackmail me with my wife."

We got money for our cans at the recycling plant. Then, as usual if Tyrone was along, I drove straight across the road to the liquor store, How Sweet It Is. There, Tyrone used the money he had just made on empty aluminum cans to purchase aluminum cans filled with malt liquor, raising the question which came first, the chicken or the egg?

Tyrone sipped at a can of malt liquor as we headed for home.

We waited for a light to change beside Foxy's Dine and Dance. The crude handpainted sign over Foxy's door declared, "WE HAVE IT ALL." Surrounding this assertion were a sign painter's renderings of All: a chain of eighth notes dashing excitedly up a scale, a hyper-curvaceous black woman in a bikini and spike heels, a billiard ball, and a mug of sudsy golden beer. The identical dimensions of the four items suggested qualitative equivalence.

"I ain't been to Foxy's in a long time," Tyrone mused.

"I was there last Saturday night," I said, deadpan.

"Tss, tss, tss, tss, tsss... You think like a black man... But now don't let it get no longer, you put me out of business."

I didn't fathom this last remark until later. He had referred to a common difference in black and white penises: the former longer and chunkier in a relaxed state than the latter (one source of the myth of the black man's superior potency), the latter more expansive in a state of excitement than the former. Tyrone's point seemed to be that if I had a black man's penis that also expanded dramatically, I'd wipe out the competition.

When I got back home, the mail that had arrived included the current issue of *PSS (Penny Stock Smarts)*.

I sat on my front porch looking through the magazine. This month's featured stock was Horizontal Drilling, a company applying new computer-related technologies (especially horizontal drilling) to aging oil and gas wells, to extract additional yields from them. The capital required to launch such an enterprise was relatively small, and HD had the backing of a Tennessee-based oil company which owned a number of the properties to be redrilled. The stock was being offered at forty-six cents a share. *PSS* thought the company "target" of two dollars a share by year's end was plausible.

Five hundred dollars would buy a thousand shares of HD stock. Buying HD shares would be consistent with the current outlook of my penny stock guru, Merlin LeClair, who thought the next great investment fortunes would be made in natural resources: oil, gas, precious and base metals. The industrialization of the Third World was sure to produce a dramatically increased demand for these commodities.

New York Doll was coming down Jackson. Noticing me on my porch, she broke out into a skip and a song. "Heigh-ho, heigh-ho, it's off to work I go…"

"All you need is a hat with a feather, and some pointy shoes," I said.

She came up on the porch and perched on the railing. I had intended the next time I saw her to complain about those damaged coins she passed off on me. But she was in such good spirits, I didn't have the heart for it.

"You're looking well," I said.

"Yeah, been eating right at my sister's all week. No crack."

"I didn't know you had a son, Doll."

"Who told you that?"

"It was in that last 'Report from the Street' you gave me."

"Oh yeah."

"Do you ever seen him?"

"My ex won't let me. He has custody."

She looked down the street, pensive suddenly. "Five years ago, I had a husband, a son, a house, a car, a job. People would say, 'Girl, you have it all.'"

"You didn't agree?"

"Bored all the time."

"That was when you got on crack?"

"Booze first, then crack."

"Well, at one time I was a college professor making decent money. That was pretty boring, too. There were four hundred applicants for a job I walked away from."

"But you didn't become an addict. You're a spiritual man."

She dug in her handbag. "Got another report for you. Wrote it last winter, then forgot to give it to you."

"What'll it cost me?"

"Two cold ones."

I got two cans of beer from the fridge. She dropped them into her big handbag, and handed me what she had written.

"Gotta get to work.... Gotta special on blow jobs this week."

"Oh, I'm a little short until payday," I said—an old joke between us. She grinned, and went off down the street.

REPORT FROM THE STREET

Well, another fuck-up morning in the land of crack cocaine, and nothing's changed. I just got in about 5:30 A.M. My new roomie has the same fuck-up attitude I left him with last night. He's been off crack three days and thinks he's cured. Don't make me laugh. He's an addict, he just don't admit it.

Yeah, as an addict, you tend not to. Been there, done that. Crack's a funny drug. Makes you feel everything is cool. Takes you down slow but sure. I'm depress as I write this, Mr. Author. You can probably tell. I won't go into details, it's self-explanatory.

Every time I think how life treats you when you do crack, I want to get rid of myself, but I don't have the nerve to do that. If it wasn't for my sister, I might have slashed my wrists New Year's Eve. That was the night I was raped at knifepoint on a billiard table.

Since I got on crack, I have been in jail four times, and homeless, mostly. I continue to hurt myself. I tell you, I would not give crack cocaine to my worst enemy. I say that, but I was the one who gave it to my mother in Harlem first, and she died using it. We had an argument right before she died. She started calling me names. I said things. I told her, if she died, don't bother calling me.

Well, she did die, and I didn't even slow down long enough to go to her funeral. It hurts me so bad, because now I can never apologize. I think I have to go to her grave in NY and beg her to forgive me.

This life is not good for me, I know for a fact. Doing crack, you have no friends, only "crack partners," as they are call. You make a lot of enemies. People in the street will give you money to keep you buying drugs, but try asking for money to buy food. No way! They rather humiliate, slander, plain cuss you out. Make you feel like shit.

But the Lord is my shepherd, I shall not want. It's up to him to save me, if anybody's going to do it, and He can, because He is all-powerful.

At four, I put the ten-cheese lasagna into the oven.

Forty years ago, when I was a newspaper delivery boy in small town Ohio, one of my customers had been an elderly Mrs. Case who lived in a windowless, pyramid-shaped attic room at Mrs. Lavery's. The room overheated in all seasons. I would go up to her room on a creaky flight of wooden steps Saturday mornings to "collect" for the week's papers. Mrs. Case might as well have lived in a shoe, for all the ventilation her room afforded. The place had a characteristic rank odor I attributed to Mrs. Case's not having washed her nether parts or her linen very often. The smell of the ten-cheese lasagna as it heated in the oven was precisely that of the old woman's room.

"My god, what's that smell?" said Hester, coming into the house from work.

"The ten-cheese lasagna.... Remember, cheese which smells awful can taste fine."

"Let us pray," Hester said.

After I had told her about Shit Boy's skulduggery in the street, she had gone to the Hoodoo-Hindoo Supply House on Margaret Mitchell Street downtown and described Shit Boy's spell for the black proprietress. The woman said the full moon tonight would be propitious for performing the "uncrossing trick," and supplied Hester medicine jars filled with the requisite sulfur dust, graveyard dirt, and chimney soot. After dinner, Hester intended to weave a counter-spell.

She removed the baking dish containing the lasagna from the oven, placed it on the counter, and pulled back foil. We peered inside. The pasta had vanished completely in a bubbling cheese bog. Poking an exploratory fork into the stuff, Hester struck something solid, and extracted a hunk of cheese-coated something that she sniffed.

"Pork sausage," she said.

She dished out the stuff, and we carried our plates to the dining room table.

"Say cheese," I said.

We each took a bite, rose immediately from our chairs without a word, walked into the kitchen with our plates and dumped their contents into a garbage bag. Hester turned on the oven again, and extracted from the refrigerator a frozen pizza.

Someone was knocking at our front door.

It was Mike, one of the roomers at Tyrone's. "I'm so hungry, I don't know what I'm gonna do," he said in a comic falsetto—a parody of the hungry man he actually was.

"Do you like lasagna?"

His eyes brightened.

"Be right back," I said.

I put the rest of the lasagna on a paper plate and covered it with foil.

"Feels like a brick," Mike said, as I handed him the package.

"It will stick to your ribs."

"If gettin' dinner here that easy, I come by every night."

"Don't press your luck."

"I hear you buyin' stories."

"Who told you that?"

"New York Doll."

"I've bought some stuff from her."

"Buy stuff from me?"

"I might, if it's good."

"Talk to you later. I gotta go eat this, before I faint."

As the full moon came into view over the treetops on the eastern horizon, Hester, Ph.D., daughter of the Enlightenment, knelt on the walk in front of our house. Wielding a cold chisel from my tool chest, she engraved small crosses in each angle of Shit Boy's large cross.

Then, sitting on our porch steps, she mixed in a sauce pan the ingredients purchased at Hoodoo-Hindoo, along with nine straight pins, and some crumbled oak leaves. She struck a match and set the concoction afire, generating a sulfuric effluvium powerful enough to scatter any demons that might have survived the ten-cheese lasagna.

Wilson stepped out of his house and raised his nostrils into the air.

Wonder Woman in her blue Spandex came by, going her

ids, and after a while Kevin strode up Jackson en route from and to Wherever.

"Hear Tyrone got twelve bucks off his cans," he called to me from the street.

"Yeah, he did."

"He said it only took half-hour. That there's twenty-four dollars an hour."

"Well, yes, if you don't count the time it took him to collect the cans."

"She-it, his time ain't worth nothin'."

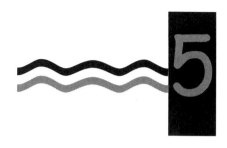

WAS GETTING INTO MY CAR in front of our house when Tom Payne hailed me from across the street. "Hey, man, Shark says y'all think I stole your fern."

"He said you had one."

"I got that fern off New York Doll. I didn't know it was yours."

"It may not have been."

But I rather thought, now, that probably it had been.

"I sold it, man."

"No big deal."

"I got it off New York Doll."

"So you said."

"All right then." He went on down the street.

I had to pick up some of Hester's academic uniforms at the dry cleaner, but before I did that, I needed to get gas for the car at the Amoco station on Boulevard up near I-20.

The sight that met my eyes at Boulevard and Glenwood filled me with dread: All that was left of Amoco were elevated concrete islands on which gas tanks had stood. The red and blue steel canopy over the islands was a wreck of twisted metal on the ground. The convenience store had vanished. A tall crane with a wrecking ball dangling from its boom, God's yo-yo, stood on the spot where the store used to be. The carwash on the back lot was a pile of concrete blocks.

I surmised what had happened. After the recent rash of robberies at Amoco, and at the Chevron station on the other side of the freeway—a night clerk had been murdered in a holdup attempt at the latter—Amoco had decided the neighborhood was too dangerous a place to do business and was pulling out! I would not have imagined the disappearance of a service station from the American landscape could affect me so powerfully. But if the 'hood was too dangerous a place for Amoco to do business, how long would the drugstore, the dry cleaner, the hobby shop, the chiropractor, Dog World, and the Avon office remain? Amoco's abandonment of that corner foretold the approaching end of civilization as we knew it.

On the way back home from the dry cleaner, I averted my eyes from the Amoco ruins. Light rain was falling. On a whim, instead of going straight down Boulevard to Jackson as I would ordinarily, I took the long way home, turning the car into Grant Park and driving its meandering roads.

I saw, from a distance, Kevin. He was standing on a curb beneath an umbrella. I honked the car horn. He looked my way, but pretended he hadn't seen me. Selling drugs again, obviously. It occurred to me that it was the first of July, and drug activity was especially lively around the first of each month when the welfare checks arrived, as it was also on the fifteenth when food stamps came out. People traded the stamps for drugs. Our tax dollars at work.

Leaving the park by the south exit, I drove a short distance on down Boulevard, turned into Jackson, and had started downhill to my house when I noticed two men standing in the Jackson-Sycamore intersection. One was a strongly-built, shirtless white man with a tangle of wet sandy hair falling to his shoulders, the other a reedy black man wearing a baseball cap and a baggy white T-shirt with a big numeral 13 on its front. They were positioned there to sell drugs obviously.

I felt it imperative I do something now to stop this contagion. I braked my car near the intersection where the two were standing, and sat there shooting poison from my basilisk eye at them. This was oddly effective. The black man retreated with studied nonchalance to the porch of a small red brick house at the corner, a rental property I had not previously associated with drug activity. The sandy-haired man, avoiding my gaze, walked up the hill on Jackson past my car. In my car's rearview mirror, I saw him disappear down alongside Tyrone's rooming house.

Back home, I telephoned our police precinct to report what I had just seen. The gruff voice of Officer Jewel who answered the phone was as clearly a black man's, as mine was a white's.

"Yeah, so what do you want us to do?" Jewel said.

The enthusiasm with which the precinct embraced information helpful citizens supplied was always so gratifying.

"You still there?" Jewel said into my silence.

"Somewhat," I said.

"Somewhat?" Jewel said, chuckling genially. "Somewhat?"

"I don't know what I want you to do, Jewel. It seems as if something might be possible. I mean, that's your business, isn't it?"

"You know where they hide their stuff?"

"How would I know that?"

"Well, how would we know it?... You seen 'em deal?"

"No, but obviously that's what they were doing. Why else would they be standing on a corner in the rain the first of the month? Why would they have reacted to me as they did?"

"Yeah, but ain't no judge gonna listen to talk like that."

"We're not in a court of law, I'm reporting suspicious activity."

"Look, man, we don't do investigative work. You'll have to call Narcotics for that."

My neighbors and I had had this run-around before. Police at the precinct would say, "Call Narcotics"; Narcotics would say, "Call the Red Dogs," the police unit specializing in gang-activity and street-dealing; and the Red Dogs would say, "Call 911." The 911 operator would say, "Call your precinct." The idea seemed to be to keep people on this merry-go-round until, dizzy and exhausted, they fell off.

"Look," I said, "kids are selling drugs in the park and on the street at night. We've got an illegal rooming house a block from my house selling crack 24-7. They have a regular staff of prostitutes. Guys hanging on a street corner first of the month strikes me as damned suspicious."

"Me, too," Jewel said. "Question is, what can you or I do about it? They probably don't have their stuff on 'em. We can't go up and down the street kicking in doors to find it. That ain't the American way. And I haven't got a guy I can send over there to spend all afternoon going through the shrubs."

"Shrubs?"

"Street dealers will hide their stuff in shrubbery. You

might find something interesting in yours."

Mzz Grant and Mzz Homer had reported seeing teenagers poking around in the box hedges between Mzz Boardman's property and mine late one night recently.

"If you want," Jewel said, "I can send a squad car over there and probably scare the guys off the corner. But that won't solve your problem."

"Yes, I'd like you to send somebody over," I said.

"I'll do that. But you need to talk to Narcotics. They get so many calls, they can't possibly handle 'em all. But keep buggin' 'em til they listen to you."

I thought I might like Jewel, if I knew him.

I called Narcotics. The woman who answered the phone said, "They come in around four."

"What's the best time to reach an investigator?" I asked.

"Four to four-fifteen, in through there—before they're out in the streets."

A narrow window, as they say. I left my number and requested a call from an investigator. Then I fetched my anti-hoodoo straw broom and went to the front of the house. There was no one up at the corner where the two men had been earlier. I swept my front walk with a frenetic vigor.

A black colleague of Hester's raised on St. Simon's Island off the Georgia coast where hoodoo practices abounded had confirmed what Mzz Grant had told me: Black folks' sweeping was a way to fend off evil influences. An advantage of sweeping frequently would be that our black neighbors would know exactly what we were doing, and would wonder what else we might be doing.

A recent media story out of New Orleans had described voodoo doctors' success in repelling drug dealers. Was that a line of resistance we should be exploring?

I swept my sidewalk from the high end of my property toward the low end. When I turned to go back uphill, New York Doll, the alleged fern-thief, was hobbling down Jackson with the assistance of an aluminum crutch. As she came closer, I saw that her face was bruised and swollen. She wore over one eye a shallow black plastic cup held in place by elastic strapped over her head, and she carried in her free hand a video-cassette recorder.

"What happened, Doll?"

"Don't want to talk about it. Hold this a minute, will you?" She handed me the VCR. Digging into her big purse, she came out with pages of loose-leaf notebook paper folded lengthwise, a new "Report from the Street."

"It's all in there," she said. "You see that skinny black guy up at the corner just now?"

"Yes."

"Midnight Marvin. He just got out of jail. Watch yourself, that man can take the hair off your head without you know it happen. He can eat the biscuit without the grease."

I tried to hand her back the VCR.

"It's yours for twenty dollars," Doll said.

"I don't want a VCR."

"You already have one?"

"No."

"Why not?"

"I don't watch movies."

"Why not?"

"Too intense. They carry me too far from myself."

"That's what I like about them... Ten."

"I don't want it, Doll."

The outrage on her battered face was that of a baby ready to throw a tantrum, a spoonful of food having been denied.

"Did you steal a fern from my porch?"

"Steal your fern?" Her oval mouth expressed total astonishment.

"Tom Payne said you gave him a fern the other night."

"Shark was the one had the fern."

The investigation of the case of the filched fern had come full circle, Shark to Shark. Merry-go-round number two.

Midnight Marvin came out of the red brick house up at the corner.

I walked away from New York Doll.

"You're in a bad mood," she muttered, continuing on her way down the hill.

Midnight Marvin gazed at me defiantly.

From my walk, I stared back at him defiantly, my broom on my shoulder, a rifleman in the straw brigade. The intensity of this staring match was such that Midnight Marvin did not notice the squad car coasting downhill silently behind him. When it drew up alongside him, he lurched as if he had been shot.

A black officer got out of the car and talked briefly with Marvin, before getting back in the car and driving off again. Marvin, making his way onto the porch of the red brick house, lifted into the air for my benefit a mighty, quivering middle finger.

I was in the house cleaning frenetically the long-neglected Venetian blinds to the accompaniment of Khachaturian's dazzling "Saber Dance" on the stereo, when I thought I heard through blaring brass and pounding drums someone knocking at our front door. I froze.

By the time I had mustered the courage to go to the front of the house and look out a window, a burly black man wearing white coveralls and white hightop sneakers whom I had never seen before was leaving my yard. I watched him until he entered Midnight Marvin's small red house. I was trembling. I was still looking over the top of window shutters into the street when a light gray van driven by a black man wearing a white skullcap came down the hill slowly. The van paused directly in front of our house. The driver stared intently toward my windows for some time before the van went on downhill. Embossed in white on the black spare tire cover at the back of the van were the words GOD-FATHER VANS, and the image of an Al Capone-era tommygun. The van made a U-turn at the foot of the hill and came back up past my house slowly. The driver again stared toward my windows. A crony of Midnight Marvin's? Of the guy in white coveralls? Of the new tenants at 533 Jackson? Were they all in cahoots?

Euripides inquired if I remembered King Pentheus in his play, *The Bacchae,* torn limb from limb by bacchantes while trying to preserve civil order from dionysian riffraff. I remembered him all too well.

Our kitchen faucet was dripping. It had been dripping for days, but not in the insidious way it was dripping just then. The drip was the agonizing, echoic, slow drip of Chinese torture. It seemed essential that this dripping be stopped now. Yes, I must go to a hardware store at once to purchase a replacement washer. I left my house and started for my car. The heavens were leaking again. I looked over the top of my Honda as I reached for the door handle, and saw the Godfather van, partially camouflaged by shrubbery, at the

Oak-Jackson intersection below my house. The driver's white skullcap was visible through foliage. My mouth went bone dry—a physiological response to fear I had never experienced in my life but must have been a part of my equipment for living from the beginning.

"Have a nice day," Bill Clinton said from his cage on Wilson's porch.

I decided against a trip to the hardware store. Instead, I walked to the back of my house, removed a pair of hedge-clippers from the crawl-space there, and launched into some hyperactive wet-weather hedge-trimming. I had been at this work for some time, whistling "Saber Dance," and had begun to feel the master of my destiny, the captain of my soul, when at my back I heard *boing-boing-boing-boing-boing*—and looked over my shoulder into the gleaming manmade smile of Shark Cryder. The Shark has pretty teeth, dear.

"Why don't you let old Shark help you with that?"

"I'd have to pay you, Shark."

"Shoot, man, I'm dirt-cheap. Do that whole hedge there for ten dollar."

"You want to deprive me of my exorcis...exercise?"

"Man you could sit back, have a cold one, and watch old Shark sweat!"

Trouble with old Shark sweating, he was likely to be casing your house meanwhile.

"New York Doll said you stole my fern."

"Like I said, Tom Payne had that fern....Did I give you one of my cards?"

He had given me five or six of his cards. He gave me another and went on his way down the alley.

RUSSELL E. (SHARK) CRYDER
General Handyman
Call today for that job tomorrow!

Nice ambiguity in "job."

I walked to the front of the house. The drizzle had stopped, the clouds dissipated, and the sun was out. The Godfather van had left the corner of Jackson and Oak. Happy times were here again. Uphill, the man in the white coveralls who had been at my address was now in front of the red brick house at Jackson and Sycamore loading equipment into a pickup truck. In bright sunlight he seemed an innocuous Mr. Clean. It was important that I find out why he had been at my house. I started up the hill, concentrating so intently on the man in white that I failed to notice Corinne Boardman lying in wait for passers-by near her gargantuan flowering mulberry. She sprang and sank verbal claws in me.

"Mr. Bottoms, he used to live where you do—he was the keeper for Willie the Gorilla over at the Zoo—Mzz Bottoms—Bouncy they used to call her—used to say he and that gorilla were like brothers."

I pressed on up the hill.

"Were you at my door earlier?" I said to the man in coveralls. "I didn't get to the door in time."

I detected, I thought, a trace of insolence in his smile.

"Johnny Chambers sent me to paint your eaves. I came to tell you I'd done the work today, except for the rain."

Reroofing my house back in the spring, Chambers had installed some new decking whose exposed underside required painting. He had promised to send a painter.

"You have other work up this way, I gather?"

Again, the insolence in his smile. He nodded toward the red brick house. "Painting walls."

There was no paint whatsoever on his coveralls.

The way back to my house led ineluctably past Mzz Boardman's house. She knew that as well as I did, and was waiting for me.

"Of course, I haven't seen Mr. Bottoms now in years," she continued. "The last time was over at South DeKalb Mall. Tawana used to take me over there to shop. She's that little colored girl lives with her sister on Confederate?… She's so sweet. We used to sit on my porch and talk and talk. I don't see her much any more, now that she has the baby. And she's working, too, of course."

New material spliced into the Bottoms tape. "Tawana got married?" I inquired innocently. Mzz Boardman's hearing had its limitations, but my sense was she had heard what I just said.

"I'll never know why they painted their house chartreuse," she replied. "Well, it's an improvement. But I always liked a nice white house with gray trim."

I took a couple steps toward my house.

Like a skilled comedienne sensing restiveness in her audience, she changed the subject abruptly. "Those bachelors in the Mather place keep to themselves, don't they?"

She referred to Don and Lee. Since I had last heard anyone use the old-fashioned term "bachelor," the phrase "gay bachelor" had taken on a whole new set of associations.

I took several more steps toward my house.

Mzz Boardman said, "In the last two months, six people in our congregation have died. Can you imagine? Six!"

Yes, I could imagine. The average age of her congregation was about seventy-five. I dove through my front door.

I now knew, more or less, who the man in the coveralls was. (Had I only imagined his insolence?) But what about the fellow driving the Godfather van? I paced restlessly from the front to the back, to the front to the back, of my house thinking about the events of that afternoon. I glanced at the clock in the dining room. It was 4:10.

I put in a telephone call to Narcotics. "They're all out in the streets," said the woman who answered the phone. A narrow window. I left another message requesting a call from an investigator.

The business section of the Atlanta *Constitution* lay on the dining room table. I picked it up and opened to the over-the-counter stock listings. Horizontal Drilling in boldface print in the "Biggest Gainers" column! The stock had gone up a dime yesterday. I must take control of my economic future without delay! I phoned my customer service representative at Charles Scrip discount brokers.

"Mr. Natural Resources, hello!" Heidi said.

"Buy me a thousand shares of Horizontal Drilling, symbol HDG."

I could hear her fingers flickering over the keyboard of her computer terminal.

"More penny stock, eh?"

"Yes."

"I can't buy that for you until you've brought me a money order. It's company policy."

"OK, I'll be in."

It would not hurt to sweep my walk again, I thought. I walked toward the front of the house with the broom.

Through the shutters at the front windows, I saw—or thought I saw—is there a difference?—the mailwoman's hand depositing mail in my box. But when I went out onto the porch, the mailbox was empty. A heavyset black woman—not the mailwoman—was going up the street with papers in her fist. Mail theft had been common on the Southside lately. I went down the porch steps and into the street. "Hey!" I called after the woman, "did you just steal my mail?"

She turned to face me. Big, dark, frightened eyes, as I walked toward her.

"What's that in your hand?"

I glimpsed briefly how some men get control over their lives by beating up women. She opened her hand to show me a paperback romance novel. On the cover, a fellow with flowing blond hair wearing a white blouse with flared sleeves was evidently just about to rip the prom gown from a swooning, rubicund, lass with exemplary hair conditioner. I exploded in laughter.

Hahahahahahahahahahaha.

Tears were welling in my eyes. It was the laughter of Dostoevsky's mad Russians.

"Are you all right, sir?" the black woman said, genuine concern showing on her face.

That she would say this just now struck me as droll in the extreme—*hahahahahahahahahahahahahahahaha*—because I had often noticed how in television police dramas or sitcoms when characters passed through some trying circumstance or other (as they do pretty often) other characters would nearly always ask: "Are you all right?"

"Hey!" Mzz Grant called from Mzz Homer's porch

across the street, "What's so funny over there?"

"Poor man can't stop laughing," said the black woman. Infected by proximity to my laughter, she herself was tittering.

"Kick him!" Mzz Grant recommended.

The part of me not in stitches, curiously aloof from the part that was, contemplated my neighbor Wilson's mailbox. Wilson was a catalogue junkie whose mailbox invariably overflowed after a mail delivery. But the box was empty. The mail had probably not arrived.

Getting myself under control again, I said to the woman, "You seem familiar. Do you live around here?"

"I used to stay up to Tyrone's," she said. "I remember you was nice, let us cut through your yard."

"Why were you on my porch just now?"

"I wanted to borrow a dollar-fifty for the bus. I gotta go downtown, see about a job."

"You knocked at my door?"

She nodded yes.

I hadn't heard anyone knocking, but I might have been at the back of my house. And because the mail arrived usually at about that hour, I might have only imagined seeing her hand in my mail box as she left the porch.

"I'll give you a dollar-fifty," I said.

I went into the house and returned with an assortment of pocket change. She was on my porch now, near the door. When I opened the screened door and reached around it to hand her coins, one dime fell through the fingers of her right hand to the porch.

"Left-handed," she explained. "Right one never did work very well."

She went into a crouch to look for the coin. I spied it on my side of the partially-opened door, and knelt to retrieve it. My knee bumped the door frame and nudged it outward slightly. The frame made contact with her knee. Delicately balanced as she was, squatting, she went over backward and sat down on the porch floor.

We were both laughing as I stepped out onto the porch and offered her my hand, which she took. My tug brought her back to her feet abruptly, and we fell into an embrace briefly. Her aura was furnace-like, as if her slate-gray skin had stored millennia of sunlight. Up close, she seemed as alien to my white kind as a member of another species.

I picked up the dime and placed it on her open palm. "Sorry I was mean," I said. "We have so many con-artists working around here…"

"You just being careful," she said. "That's smart. There are a lot of crazy folks around here."

"What's your name?" I asked the woman.

"Betty."

"If you take the bus downtown, Betty, how will you get home?"

"Walk, probably."

"Where do you live?"

"Summerhill."

"That's a long walk from downtown." I took from my wallet two dollar bills and gave them to her. "For the ride home."

She gave my arm an appreciative squeeze. "Pay you back Friday."

I wouldn't hold my breath. I had been repaid for these "loans" only once over the years—by John the Drunk.

Shortly after we moved into the neighborhood he had one night borrowed five from me. Drunk the next night, he came to my door to repay his debt.

Drunk the night after that, he tried to repay me a second time.

I picked up Doll's new "Report from the Street."

A BAD EXPERIENCE

Last night, my so-called friend Tyrone invited me to have a drink with him in his room. We had our drink, and he gave me $5 to buy a hit, which I did, and smoked it. I went back to his room later, and he invited me to have another drink. He kept giving me drinks out of a bottle of corn liquor. I noticed he wasn't drinking much, a little Ernest and Julio's white wine was all. But I had no idea he was setting me up for the kill.

I don't know what I said made him snap. I was pretty high. All of a sudden he started beating me with his cane. He hits me again and again. I kept putting my arms up so I wouldn't get a black eye, and he kept hitting me.

I was trying to get out of the door, but he came right behind me, and hit me with the cane on my back. I fell down. He hit me some more while I was lying there, and for the first time ever, I thought I might be about to meet my Maker. When I got up again, he grabbed me by the neck and rammed my face into the corner of the cupboard. That was when my eyelid split. I heard it go POP.

I had to have stitches in my eyebrow at Grady, and I am schedule to have my eyelid put back together next week. I am fucked-up.

Last night, I kept dreaming of the dead. I dreamed about my Grandma dying in her bed. Tyrone was sitting on a chair beside her. A woman I know told me if you dream like that, it's from the devil, and you are going to die.

MY PREPARATION FOR SLEEP on summer nights consisted sometimes of an aimless perambulation of house and yard. I paused in this soporific strolling of mine one night to switch on the television set and watch a somniferous inning of a game between the Atlanta Braves and the Chicago Cubs, before ambling out onto our side porch at the front of the house.

Wonder Woman came down the hill, her belt-purse swagging with its heavy contents. Over on Oak Street, the basketball was hitting the pavement. A wine-red van that made regular drug-delivery stops in the 'hood stopped in front of a house down the street. A man left the van and went down along the side of the house to the back.

"Gas man," he called. Someone laughed.

Mookie, a black prostitute-addict, whose long thin legs coupled to an abundant posterior yielded world-class sashaying, came down Jackson, just as another prostitute, Simone, was coming uphill. The two women met under the streetlight in front of my house.

Mookie said, "I ran out of Vaseline, and I'm using chicken grease. Do I smell?"

"Girrrrl!" Simone said, laughing, "You crazy if you think I'm gonna get close enough to find out!"

A battered old green Mercedes came down Jackson, bass music booming from speakers in its hollow trunk: *Dadada DOOOOOM!* . . . . . *Dadada DOOOOOM!* . . . . . *Dadada DOOOOOM!*

The Mercedes paused beside the two women. Negotiations ensued. Mookie got into the car, Simone went on up the hill.

I walked the length of my house front to back, and exited the back door. I walked along the side yard back toward the front of the house, past our immobilized old Toyota. Why not just give the car to Mike and be done with it? He repaired cars and might be able to get it going again. If not, he could make a few dollars selling it for parts, or as scrap. Yes, that was what I would do.

I leaned against my Honda in the driveway for a while. A black man wearing a white baseball cap that glowed in the dark had positioned himself up at the Sycamore-Jackson intersection where Midnight Marvin had been the other day. I stared at the man prolongedly.

He came down the hill past me. "Got change for a twenty?" he said.

"Sorry, no," I said, pretending innocence of the subtext: *Tit-fo-tat, muthafuka.*

He walked on down Jackson toward Confederate.

Back in the house again, I gazed at shelves of books I rarely read anymore. At one time it had seemed to me I might learn from books how to conduct my life wisely, my culture not having been of much help with that. I had assumed foolishly that there was a way to live wisely, *in situ,* if

I could just figure out what it was.

Among the books was a condensation of Arnold Toynbee's multi-volume *A Study of History*. Toynbee's work had always bored me. But I took the volume down, blew a little dust off the top, and opened at random to a passage on the social destructiveness of marauding proletarian bands that was, in fact, very interesting.

What had been characteristic of proletariats throughout history, Toynbee wrote, was "neither poverty nor humble birth, but a consciousness—and the resentment this consciousness inspired—of being disinherited from…place in society." Often the source of that consciousness had been the failure of a dominant minority to look after the needs of society's defenseless lower classes *(Noblesse oblige)*. A disinherited, disaffected rabble was capable of an "explosion of savagery which surpasses in violence the cruelty of their oppressors and exploiters."

The security alarm at Wilson's house went off.

These house alarms cried wolf too often. I was ignoring the sound, when Hester came running into my study. "Somebody just kicked in Wilson's porch door and stole his bicycle! Kevin saw the whole thing. He's at the front door."

"Is Wilson home?"

"No."

I dropped Toynbee to the floor. Hastening to the front door of the house, I ushered Kevin inside, tapped 911 into the telephone, and handed it to him. "Tell the operator just what you saw."

Kevin did so with, for him, surprising directness and clarity: A black man wearing a white baseball cap had kicked in Wilson's door and ridden off down Jackson toward Confederate Avenue on Wilson's bicycle.

"Sumpin wrong with the wheel of the bike," Kevin said. "Didn't steer good."

Kevin, Hester and I went onto the front porch. Two squad cars, blue lights flashing, swept down Jackson past our house. At Confederate, one went south, one north, and it was not long after that the 911 operator called to say that the "perpetrator" had been caught red-handed with the goods—Wilson's bike and his power saw. The getaway had not been expeditious, because the bicycle had a flat tire.

"We kicked butt!" Kevin exulted. We exchanged high-fives. Tonight, at least, he was on our side. He galloped down the hill to Oak Street to tell Maggie Spitz what had happened.

I lingered on the front porch for a while. It was getting on toward midnight when the front door up the street at 533 Jackson opened. A figure silhouetted by the light from an interior room who appeared to look my way hesitated in the doorway, then shut the door and started up the hill.

Curious about what his destination at that late hour might be, I waited a few minutes, and then got in my car and drove up to Boulevard. A few blocks north of Jackson on Boulevard I caught sight of him. I drove past him slowly, and then circled around behind him. I passed him a second time, and a third, and a fourth, before finally losing track of him up near the freeway.

The next morning, I drove out to a building supply warehouse. A knowledgeable clerk in the electronics department described for me the two kinds of home security systems, monitored and unmonitored. The hardware was the same in either case: magnetic sensor switches on doors and windows to detect attempts at forced entry, and infrared motion detectors to respond to bodies moving through the interior of a house. Once activated, these devices triggered a blaring siren mounted on the exterior of a house, to startle intruders and alert neighbors. If the system were monitored by a security company, which charged a monthly fee for its services, a telephone call went to the police 911 emergency system. Theoretically, the cops would soon be on the scene.

However, the ingenuous clerk confirmed the scuttlebutt that these systems were not without quirks and failings. False alarms were common. A stiff wind moving a door or window slightly in its frame, or a cat in a windowsill lurching against a window pane during a flea-attack, could activate the sensor-switches. A bored ten year-old boy could enliven his neighborhood considerably on a midsummer night by putting a shoulder into the back door of the Jones' house while the Joneses were on vacation. The infrared motion detectors responded not only to burly home-invaders, but to scampering mice, thermal currents accompanying dramatic weather changes, and hot air issuing from forced air heating vents—not to mention the homeowner who forgets his system is operative and ventures into its field of coverage.

And at times, the alarms seemed at times to go off for no reason at all. The clerk speculated that ghosts, whose love of tinkering with electrical circuitry and appliances was well-documented, probably found home security systems irresistible.

Even if a house alarm went off for the right reasons, a significant response in the middle of the night from awakened neighbors weary of false alarms—other than gnashing of the teeth—was unlikely. A timely response from Atlanta's sorely overburdened and shorthanded police force was about equally improbable.

Thanking the clerk for his candor, I told him I would think about the matter further. It seemed as if purchasing a home security system might be more fetishistic than practical.

I drove from the building supply store to Lenox Square, and entered Charles Scrip's offices, money order in hand. My customer service rep Heidi smiled from her cubicle and beckoned to me. She brought up my account on her computer screen. "Well, you aren't exactly getting rich with your contrarian investing, but you seem to be holding your own."

"Preservation of capital is the crucial thing as the Greater Depression approaches," I pontificated deadpan, parroting my investment guru Merlin LeClair. Belief seems to be the automatic response of a woman to anything a man says with an appearance of conviction; and what I had just said held Heidi's wits captive for a few seconds. Eyeing the Velcro straps on my $19.99 sneakers, she got control of herself.

"So what'll it be today?" she said.

"A thousand shares of Horizontal Drilling," I said.

"Ah yes, Horizontal Drilling—how quickly we forget . . . Horizontal Drilling." Her fingers flew over her keyboard. "Horizontal Drilling . . . Horizontal Drilling . . . Come in Horizontal Drilling. Yes, here it is. They're offering at forty-five cents a share."

"Buy," I said. "It's a steal at anything under a dollar."

She again looked at me as if I might be in possession of occult knowledge.

I presented her with my money order. Her fingers flickered over the keyboard once more. Waiting for results to come up, eyes to the screen, she said, "You aren't from around here, are you?"

On my answering machine at home there was a message from Bill Avery, a young lawyer who lived on Lee Street. I punched into my telephone the number Avery had left.

"What the holy hell is going on in the neighborhood?" Avery said.

"How do you mean?"

"On Lee this week we've had a home invasion, a car theft, and a string of car break-ins... Are you having more trouble down your way?"

"No, it's been pretty quiet down here," I said. I was not sure why I lied, maybe because the way Avery said "down your way" reminded me of Dante's Inferno.

"I had no idea how extensive this drug activity has become," he said.

I had tried to tell him that back in March.

"I was driving past that rooming house up the street from you the other night, and some teenagers offered me drugs."

"I'm not too surprised," I said.

"I've talked over the situation with Commander Gardner of the Red Dogs. Jeff and I are old friends. I'm going to discuss it with Councilman Albright over lunch tomorrow."

"Good."

"Gardner wants to set up a meeting for us with a narcotics investigator. Could you turn out some people?"

"I think so, yes."

"We've got to get a handle on this situation before it gets out of control."

Exactly what I had said back in March.

"I think our first priority ought to be that rooming house," Avery added.

Good idea.

I telephoned Jake Macht at his office to pass along the substance of Avery's call.

"Maybe your telling Kevin the Lee Street people were behind the police sweeps is paying off," Jake said, laughing.

"That evil thought did cross my mind."

"So Avery's decided he needs us after all.... Maybe we should play hard to get."

"No, I think we'd better play ball with anyone willing to get involved, especially if he has political connections, as Avery does."

I was aware of having made the not necessarily valid assumption that if criminal activity originated when people were not involved, it would cease once they were. "Getting involved" tended, in my experience, to yield mainly a quantity of pronouncements and gestures. It resembled, a bit, buying a home security system. Symbolic actions increased in psychological importance about in proportion as existential problems were insoluble.

"That African Methodist Episcopal Church down the street from me was burglarized again the other night," Jake said.

"What's that, the third time?"

"Third or fourth."

"I wonder if the congregation would be willing to work with us?"

"It would be worth asking."

"I'll make it my civic duty for the week to get in touch with them."

"Good man... I was driving down Jonesboro Road the other morning about ten. For about a mile and a half south of the Capitol, there were gangbanger types on every street corner, eight or ten to a pack. Incredible scene."

"What were they doing?"

"Don't ask me. I've never seen anything quite like it—not in this country. It looked like Mexico City."

"Did you call the precinct?"

"I talked to Captain Turnipseed. He said they were aware of the situation."

I laughed—and explained why I was laughing: Those had been Turnipseed's exact words to me after a public safety meeting at a local church last winter at which I had been outspoken about police neglect of drug activity in our neighborhood. Afterward, Turnipseed, had approached me to ask where exactly I lived. When I told him, he had not lowered his face swiftly enough to prevent my seeing the smile that spread across it. He found it hilarious that a mature, articulate white man should be living where he would not himself have deigned to live. Did I really expect the criminal justice system, largely controlled by blacks in Atlanta and responsive to black political interests, to disturb the lives and livelihoods of his own race's most feckless sadsacks on behalf of an unsuccessful white man?

Turnipseed got his sense of humor under control and presented his face to my gaze once more. "We're aware of that situation," he said gravely.

"So he's aware of everything," Jake said. "Does he ever

do anything about it?"

"I don't know… By the way, the Atlanta *Constitution* is going to publish the piece I wrote about that public safety meeting."

"Good. When?"

"They haven't said."

"I'll watch for it."

"Avery thinks we ought to be targeting Tyrone's rooming house."

"So do I," Jake said. "How about you?"

"I agree. But just to play devil's advocate—supposing we bust Tyrone, then what? Fulton County Jail's so crowded, people arrested for possession of small quantities aren't even seeing judges. Solicitors work out plea-bargains and flush them right back into the streets. If the rooming house gang were arrested, they might be right back in our faces. There could be retaliation."

"If there's no punishment for getting caught, why bother retaliating?"

"Why burn someone's house down and risk getting in real trouble?"

"Yeah."

I wondered, though, if we could count on good sense to prevail over suicidal belligerence. "By the same token," I said, "if there's no punishment for getting caught, why bother arresting them in the first place?"

"Just to shake things up," Jake said. "They might think we know something they don't."

No one at Narcotics had ever responded to my calls. I

called again. The woman who answered the phone was the one I had talked with earlier.

"They never got back to you?"

"No."

"Shame on 'em! Whatcha got, hon? Maybe I can help."

I described recent street-dealing in our neighborhood.

"Y'all got a case of it, don't you? Listen, I'll have somebody call you today for sure. But I really think you need to talk to the Red Dogs. Gangs and street-dealing is their business." She gave me their number.

I phoned the Red Dogs and listened to their recorded message: "Your call is very important to us. No one is available to take your call at the moment. Please leave your number after the tone."

I left my number. Then I picked up my anti-hoodoo broom and went out the front door of the house. Sweeping, I could hear bantering voices of young black men coming from the windows at 533 Jackson up the hill.

Maggie Spitz in her battered white Chevie pickup pulled to the curb beside me. Kevin was with her. I went to the open passenger-side widow of the truck.

"Shit Boy and two of his cronies cornered me at Chevron last night," Maggie said.

"Cornered you?"

"Boxed me in with their cars so I couldn't move."

"What was the point of that?"

"Dumb shits," Kevin said.

"I stuck my Magnum out the window and told the suckers to back off," Maggie said.

"Did they?"

"Yeah… I hear Wilson got robbed the other night."

"He did. Kevin was the hero of that episode."

"So the hero's told me more than once."

"You know what Dumbo did?" Kevin said. "He said he'd give Karen two dollars if she took off her shirt and let him feel her titties." Karen was Maggie's ten year-old daughter.

"Did it upset Karen?" I asked Maggie.

"She thought it was the funniest thing she ever heard of. She's kind of immature for her age."

"Is Dumbo dangerous that way?"

"I don't know," Maggie said, "but I sure as hell don't want him hanging around my kids any more, and I told his mother that. You know what she said? 'Why, I'm just so sorry! I swear, I just don't know what to do with that boy.' I know what she can do with the boy—put him in a goddamn institution."

"Maggie found out who them guys over at 533 is," said Kevin, pointing up the street.

"They're supposed to be rap musicians," Maggie said. "I was driving past the house yesterday, and a woman I know came out of it. I stopped and talked to her. She's an aide in a law office, and she'd come to deliver a contract."

"So they're straight?"

"She said they recorded for some small company in Los Angeles."

"That would explain the California connection."

"Still sumpin fishy, if you ask me. Too many people coming and going all the time. Too much play, too little work."

"Who are the teenage boys wearing the white shirts?"

"Don't ask me."

"They ain't from around here," Kevin said. "Mother Grant saw sheriff's deputies over there yesterday."

"What for?" I asked.

Kevin shrugged his shoulders.

"Tell you another suspicious case," Maggie said, "is that woman moved in where the Kitchens used to be. Where's the money coming from? She doesn't work, she's always at home."

"Well, I'm usually home."

"Yeah, but I know your source of income, and you don't drive a new Lexus the way she does… She just bought that house, right? Now most people after they buy a house are pretty broke. But the department store trucks keep deliverin' new furniture. She hired an interior decorator to do the wallpaper. She had a landscaper resod her yard. I know her daughter goes to a private school, because she plays on Angie's Little League team."

"I see a guy down there sometimes. Maybe he's the sugar daddy?"

"Sure as hell looks like one in them overalls, drivin' an old Ford Escort."

"An eccentric millionaire?"

"Oh yeah, we got a slew of them around here!… Both of them were at the kids' baseball game the other night. I invited the whole team to the house for ice cream afterward. You know what? They wouldn't let the girl come."

"Hmm… Maybe the race thing?"

"Half the Orioles is black! The kids say they ought to rename their team the Oreos."

Simone came downhill, rubber thongs slapping the pavement. She had been animated and flirtatious hustling me for a dollar to buy cigarettes a week ago, but she was stony-eyed as she passed us now.

"There's one mean-lookin' bitch," Maggie mused.

"Needs a hit," Kevin said. "She's goin up to Snothead's for one now."

Kevin, looking in the truck's rearview mirror on the passenger-side door, said, "Oh-oh, here comes Tony."

I glanced downhill. Tony, a short, barrel-chested young black man was coming uphill. As he neared Simone, the gap between them widened, and they did not speak.

"I thought they were sleeping together," I said.

"Was," Kevin said, "before she caught him fuckin' her sister."

"Variety's the spice of life," I said.

"Variety's the spice of life?" Kevin repeated, slowly, this remarkable sentence and looked at me with wonder. How easily I could toss off such gems! I had also wowed him recently with "six of one, half-dozen of the other."

"I'm thinking about installing a home security system," I said.

"Don't do it, waste of money," Maggie said. "They're more trouble than they're worth. Take it from someone who has one. What you want to do is just put up a sign out front your house saying you have one. Let it go at that."

"Where do you get a sign?"

"Our system came with two, I'll give you one."

Wilson came across his lawn toward us, carrying a bow saw. "Is this yours?" he asked me. "I found it on my side of the fence."

"Tyrone's saw," Kevin said.

"Must have slipped under the fence that day he trimmed my tree," I said.

"You people will no doubt be happy to hear that I just

sold my mouthy parrot," Wilson said.

"Aw no, you didn't, Wilson?" Maggie complained.

"For shame, Wilson!" I added.

"Who Mzz Grant gonna talk to now?" Kevin said.

Wilson backed up a few steps and covered his face with his forearms. "Golly, guys, I'm sorry. If I'd known I was disrupting the neighborhood, I wouldn't have done it… He hasn't gone very far. The woman I sold him to lives right up the street."

"Well, it won't be the same," Maggie said. "I hear you got burgled, Wilson."

"Twice. I lost my bicycle and his ladder. Got the bicycle back."

"Wilson makes the mistake of leaving his house sometimes," I explained.

"You know what?" Wilson said, turning to me. "When I went down to the precinct to get my bike, a Detective Johnson interviewed me. He said the guy that stole it claimed you'd helped plan the job. I told him that was preposterous."

"What did the detective say?"

"He just laughed. Apparently that happens a lot when they pick guys up. They see it as an opportunity to get even."

Change for a twenty.

I resumed sweeping after my neighbors had gone off.

"Get all that conjure dust," Mzz Grant called from Mzz Homer's porch.

"I'm working on it."

Two vans with opaque tinted windows and California tags pulled up in front of 533 Jackson. The van horn honked. The door at 533 opened, and a swarm of black teenagers wearing identical white T-shirts, tails outside the trousers, burst into the yard.

"That's the guy," one of them said, pointing at me.

"Hey, Klu Klux Klan man!"

Several made circles of their fists and pretended to look at me through binoculars.

This close to them, I noticed something I had not before. There was a small numeral 13 printed on the left sleeve of each of their T-shirts.

"He don't like having black men this close."

"Bet his woman does!"

Hoots and snickers.

"Cool it, Scott!"

"We gotta Neighborhood Watch, honky—and we're watchin' you."

"Yeah, we gotta Honky Watch!"

Tribal hilarity as the teenagers packed themselves into the vans, which then started up the hill.

I noticed something on the sidewalk concrete I hadn't before: the faint outlines of a huge eyesocket and eyeball: the Evil Eye. It could have been engraved there by Shit Boy or one of his friends, Midnight Marvin or one of his group, the crowd at 533 across the street—or maybe some friend of the guy arrested the other night for burglarizing Wilson?

I was trembling again. Had I spent my life in Belfast or Jerusalem, attempts at intimidation as mild and furtive as this would have seemed laughable. But I had passed my life among people rendered mild by the tedium of prosperity. The fact was, I was trembling. Well, the flesh is weak. What else was new? The thing to do if weak flesh was trembling, I guessed, was to go about one's business and let it tremble on until it got tired of trembling (as it got tired of everything) and went on to something else. I resumed sweeping my walk.

I swept now with increased fervor. My impassioned left-right, left-right, left-right began to approximate dancing. "Primitive" peoples danced to dispel evil influences, work up courage for battle, etc. Was it dancing that did the trick, or just the physical exertion that dancing required? Physical exertion of nearly any kind—hammering, screwing, running, hoeing—allayed fears and boosted morale. Soldiers marched vigorously toward the scene of battle. Children, afraid of the dark, ran, not just to get out of it, but as self-defensive magic while passing through it. The fear-repellent aspect of vigorous physical activity might help account for the compulsive athleticism of the Americans on their notoriously insecure continent.

Having swept the walk twice, I went to my porch and sat down in the canvas director's chair. I put my feet up on the railing: captain of my soul, master of my fate, and a wonderfully fat target for a drive-by shooting.

The phone in the house rang.

Hester on the line with a question about our checking account balance. I told her about the Evil Eye on the sidewalk.

"Oh, I did that. Didn't I mention it? The woman at the hoodoo shop said it would scare off evil spirits. Kind of like a gargoyle."

"I wish you had mentioned it… Do you really think all this magic is going to work?"

"I don't know, it's fun… Oh, by the way, Fester and his wife were both at my bus stop this morning."

"I've never seen her before."

"She has long black hair, like Mortitia in the Addams family."

"Is she six-six and skinny?"

"No, five-two and one-eighty."

I laughed. "Was Fester behaving himself?"

"He was standing too close to me, as usual, and trying to strike up a conversation. She seemed kind of embarrassed by it. They got on the bus and rode all the way downtown. They sat on one of those long benches running parallel to the side of the bus. At one point, I looked over, and she was groping him."

Mzz Grant knocked at the front door. If I wasn't busy, could I give her a lift up to the drugstore?

I had nothing better to do.

She went up to her house on Sycamore for her purse. Whenever Mzz Grant ran out of some personal item, she would solicit a ride to a store from a neighbor with a car. Her inability to develop shopping lists and plan ahead to meet her simple needs had seemed almost pathological to me when I first moved into the 'hood. Later, I had seen a kind of method in the madness. Trips to stores were among the few opportunities she had to get out of the neighborhood and ward off what she called the "heebie-jeebies," so the fewer items she purchased on any one shopping trip, the more trips she could enjoy.

As Mzz Grant eased her weighty person into the bucket seat of the Honda, she was denouncing the City of Atlanta's new trash disposal arrangements which required citizens to separate aluminum cans, bottles, tin cans, and newspapers, from other household refuse.

"I liked the old way, dump everything together, be done

with it," she said.

"The trouble with that, Mary, is we're running out of places to put trash," I said. "And a lot of stuff we throw away, like newspapers, can be reused. It takes a lot of trees to make one Sunday newspaper. We're cutting trees to make newspapers faster than we can grow new ones."

"Who make newspapers outta trees?"

"Everyone does!" I said—with conviction enough to give her, a woman, pause. She seemed to be pondering the matter as we drove up the hill on Jackson.

I was thinking about what a former truck driver had told me recently. Every night, fragrant fleets of semis filled with baled New Jersey refuse for which there was no longer any place in that state, set out across the Pennsylvania Turnpike for landfills near Youngstown.

A red light at Jackson and Boulevard stopped us.

At our right, two unshaven black men in shabby clothes, each with an open pint bottle of wine in his hand, sat by the entrance to the lower half of a split-level house.

"Goddamnmuthafuksumbitch," the one declared, his head weaving.

"I don't give a shit what that muthafuk say," commented the other.

"Hey!" Mzz Grant called out the open car window. "Y'all need to wash your mouth out with soap!" As punctuation for this invective, she rolled up the car window smartly.

Taken aback by this unanticipated attack, the two open-mouthed men stared at her.

"Caw-caw-caw!" came a cry off to our left.

Bill Clinton sat in his cage at the open front window of

what was obviously his new home directly across the street from the two foul-mouthed men.

"Caw-caw-caw!" Mzz Grant crowed deafeningly into my right ear.

The light changed. I turned the car north up Boulevard.

"Who were those guys?" I asked.

"Homeless," Mzz Grant said. "They been sleeping in that house. Broke in through the back. I can hear 'em cussin all the way up to my house. Fuck this, and fuck that."

We had gone a little way along Boulevard toward the drug store when, to conclude our earlier discussion, Mzz Grant said she felt that separating one kind of trash from another was a whole lot of trouble, considering that the world was about to end.

I was thinking that night about the white T-shirts of the teenagers who had come out of 533 Jackson, when I recalled vaguely a passage in the Atlanta police manual on the city street gangs, "Banging Southern Style." I located the manual in my study, and found the passage in question. White, it said, was the insignia color of the Southern California-based "Sur 13" gangs said to have established a beachhead in northeast Atlanta, not far from our area. Sur 13's main business on the West Coast was dealing crack-cocaine. That inexpensive drug was the favorite currently in poor inner-city Atlanta, too.

Midnight Marvin had worn number 13 on his shirt, and so had Sparkle Plenty. According to the manual, 13 referred to the thirteenth letter of the alphabet, M, which referred, in turn, to the Mexican Mafia.

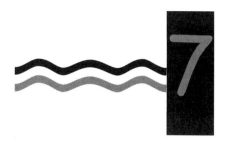

MAGGIE PUT THE MAGIC SECURITY company sign in my yard. Perhaps I should now have felt secure. But this seemed too easy. So I paid a hundred dollars for an unmonitored security system I could install myself.

It took most of an afternoon to study the installation manual, measure, drill holes, run wires, mount the siren under my front porch roof and the control unit inside my front door. Having done all this, I felt I had earned the right to feel secure.

There was a "panic button" on the control unit which activated the siren manually. The siren was directly over the front porch railing where our neighbor's tomcat Sid was sprawled asleep. I pressed the panic button, and had the pleasure of seeing the panicked Sid airborne briefly. He landed on all fours in the yard. The look he sent up at me was dour. I had the feeling I would pay eventually for this prank, one way or another.

Wednesday night that week I was driving up Boulevard to the drugstore when I noticed an old car in front of Jake Macht's house. The car listed pronouncedly, because the front and rear wheels facing the street were missing. Shattered greenish glass lay all about the car. The windows were gone.

On my return home, a cluster of black church women in wide-brimmed hats, white pumps, and colorful bold-patterned summer dresses were gabbing on the front steps of the African Methodist Episcopal Church, a small stone church at Boulevard and Lee. The Wednesday night service had just let out. I turned the car into Lee Street alongside the church. A tall, lean black man in a dark blue suit, Bible in one hand, was locking a side door. The pastor?

I pulled the Honda to the curb beside the church. There was apprehensiveness in the man's eyes as I did this. I got out of the car, approached him, and extended my right hand, which he took in his own without much enthusiasm. I introduced myself as a neighbor concerned about recent criminal activity. Was he the pastor?

No, he was assistant pastor, Willie Harrell.

"We understand your church has been burglarized lately?"

"Four times."

I described our attempts to organize resistance to criminal activity. "Would your congregation be interested in working with our group?"

He lowered his head, chuckling involuntarily. "You'd have to ask Reverend Ivey about that."

"Is he here?"

"No, he left about five minutes ago."

"Does he live nearby?"

"In Decatur."

"Could you give me his phone number?"

"I don't recall it right off, he's got a new one. If you want to give me your number, I'll have him call you."

I gave Harrell my number.

Mike came walking down Jackson one evening at twilight when I was sitting on my front porch steps. I hadn't seen him since I fed him the ten-cheese lasagna. Between then and now, he had become a bald man. He came up the walk to the edge of my porch.

"That lasagna was good," he said, "but I didn't feel too good the next day. Felt like ah had fat running outta my ears."

"You probably did."

"Filled me up, though."

"Did it make your hair fall out?"

He planted a large hand on his craggy, polished mahogany top and pointed uphill with his other hand. "A guy back there at the corner stole my hair!"

"We've got a hair thief in the 'hood?"

"Yeah!"

"Hot hair."

"Somebody try to sell you a head of hair, let me know."

"It would look good on me."

"Yeah, would."

"I know what it would cost too—five dollars."

"Folks around here, they count one, two, three, four, five—and then they kinda jump from there to ten, fifteen, twenty."

"I've noticed that."

The phone rang in the house. "Be right back."

"Hello?" I said.

"Heh-lo," said a woman's voice.

"Hello?"

"Heh-lo, heh-lo, heh-lo."

Click.

A prank. I went back outside.

"I got a story for you," Mike said.

"What's it about?"

"My suicide attempt."

"For real?"

"Yeah."

"When was this?"

"Summer of '89." He held out his arm to show me scar tissue where he had slit his wrist.

"Why'd you do it?"

"Depressed. Always been depressed a lot. Born that way, I think."

"Wrist-slitters aren't usually serious suicides."

"Well, I come pretty close to doin' the job."

He related the sequence of events that had led to his wrist-slashing.

"That would have been painful at the time," I observed, "but it's funny, looking back."

"Seems funny to me."

"You know, I might like to write that as a story, or part of one. Would you mind if I did that?"

My scruples surprised him. "I'd be honored."

"Tell you what. When you have the time, we'll sit down and go through the whole thing again, slowly and in detail, and I'll make notes."

"What the pay?"

I thought about it. "How about five dollars a session, for as many as it takes."

"OK. Not tonight, though. I gotta go up Mzz Tanner's in a little while here, try to get her car started."

"There's no rush."

"Could you advance me five?"

The phone rang in the house again.

"Hello."

"Heh-lo."

"Hello?"

"Heh-lo."

"What number are you trying to reach?"

Click.

I rejoined Mike, and advanced him five.

"After I cut my wrist," Mike said, "I did the dumbest thing I done in my whole life."

"Dumber than attempting suicide?"

"Lot dumber. You want to hear about that?"

"What's the price?"

"This here's a free sample. I'll tell you if the meter running."

"OK."

An emergency room doctor at Grady Hospital, Atlanta's inner-city charity hospital, had sewn up Mike's wrist, and given him a blood transfusion. Grady kept him several days for observation, then sent him on to a state-operated mental facility in DeKalb County for psychological evaluation and counseling.

His first night at the mental hospital, Mike's companion at a small table in the refectory was a taciturn black man with a very large head, neck, arms, gut, and thighs. Mike tried without success to start a conversation with this fellow, whose attention was fixed on a uniformed black woman standing guard at the doorway to the refectory.

After the evening meal each night, patients of both sexes could hobnob in the courtyard, and Mike was looking forward to that. Some of the women were nice-looking. One light-skinned woman with a good figure had been making eyes at him all day. The patients he had met so far had not seemed much different from people in the streets of Atlanta. The food was pretty good, the rent was free. Being crazy was not all that bad a deal. Some of the patients must have worked pretty hard at seeming crazy enough to get in here, he guessed.

His companion at the table unzipped his fly, removed his penis from his pants and began massaging it. Its dimensions were proportional to the rest of the man.

"Hey, man," Mike said, "Would you put that thing back in yo pants? I'm trying to eat my meal. You wanna make me sick?"

Three attendants, two women and a man, came running. The male guard and one of the women seized the big guy's arms. The third guard removed from the leather holster on her belt a hypodermic needle.

"She did it underhand, like pitching a softball," Mike said. "Stuck that thing in his butt right through his pants."

"Did it work?" I asked.

"Worked real good. About five seconds, and the big dude ain't feelin' no pain."

Mike folded his hands over his stomach and stared heavenward with a beatific smile, imitating the chemically-induced euphoria of the fellow.

Sam, Mike's roommate at the hospital, was another quiet one. A short, wiry, intense fellow with big luminous eyes, Sam spent much of each day pacing agitatedly around the perimeter of the central hall at the hospital while other patients watched television, played cards, or read. Sam, as he paced, engaged in what seemed to be intense dramatic monologues. Sometimes he raised his hands to his chest to shadow box.

Periodically, he would return to the room he shared with Mike.

Back in the main hall again, he would be an altered man, clicking his fingers in time to rhythms he alone heard, slapping backs, and shaking hands. "Hey, bro, howya doin'?"

Mike began to notice that during meals, Sam always filled his pockets with pink sugar envelopes from the refectory tables; and one day when Sam left the bottom drawer of his dresser ajar slightly, Mike saw it was chock-full of sugar packets.

Mike took aside one of the security guards, a black woman. "Y'all know my roommate's stealin' your sugar?"

This guard and another, an Hispanic man, went toward Sam's room to investigate Mike's claim. Sam, observing them approaching his room, followed after. When he entered the room, Mike and the Hispanic were kneeling by the dresser examining the sugar drawer.

Sam leapt on the Hispanic's back. "Y'all leave mah sugar alone! Don't you evah mess with mah sugah!"

The two men rolled around on the floor, wrestling. Sam

was the smaller of the two, but having a greater stake in the conflict fought more valiantly. He had straddled the Hispanic's stomach, and was using his forearms to press the Hispanic's arms to the floor, when the black woman unsheathed her hypodermic needle and jammed it into Sam's elevated posterior.

"They was very big on stabbin' people in the butt at that hospital," Mike said.

"I can tell," I said.

"All had that little holster on their belt, like a six-shooter."

"You were going to tell me about the dumbest thing you ever did."

"Comin' to that."

In the courtyard after dinner one night, the light-skinned woman who had been making eyes at Mike sat down beside him and introduced herself as Thrash Gordon.

"Thrash?" Mike said. "Never knowed anybody call Thrash."

"I am the one and only Thrash," she said. The name was short for "thrasher," the state bird of Georgia.

"What you in for, Thrash?" Mike asked.

"Mainly the sex," Thrash said, slapping him on the thigh.

"Y'all get sex in here?"

"I don't," Thrash said, "Friend of mine got plenty last year."

"Where the line form?" Mike said, cracking up Thrash.

"You're funny," Thrash said. "I like a man make me laugh."

"You want me to tickle you?"

"If you tickle good," Thrash said. "Been so long since I been tickled good, I'm growing cobwebs down there."

"You're funny, too," Mike said.

"I like you," Thrash said.

"I like you," Mike said.

She put her hand between his legs.

Mike glanced over his shoulder toward a pair of guards at the courtyard entrance to the hospital. "Can you do that?" he said.

"I can. You try, they stick you in the butt."

Mike's trouser zipper was old and inefficient, and Thrash was struggling with it. Other patients, intrigued by her efforts, were pointing and snickering. Mike noticed one of the guards looking his way. He got to his feet and started for his room. Some of these folks were a whole lot crazier than they looked.

The night after Thrash made her move on Mike in the courtyard, she went over the top of a twelve-foot barbed wire fence surrounding the hospital grounds. Scratched, bleeding, and topless, she was standing along I-20 a mile from the hospital waving her T-shirt at passers-by, trying to hitch a ride, when hospital security caught up with her.

Mike was at the open window of his room overlooking the service entrance at the rear of the hospital when the guards brought her back. Her clothes were torn and blood-stained.

"All I wanted was a little dick," she was muttering. "Was that too much to ask? ... All I wanted was a little dick."

Mike had been at the hospital two weeks when his counselor told him that he was free to leave any time, if he felt he could cope. If he wanted to remain at the hospital five months longer, she could arrange for him to receive regular monthly disability checks from the state.

"No m'am," he said, "just want to get back to my work."

He left the hospital that night.

"You'd had enough of the crazy people?" I said.

"Yeah."

Silence. "Dumbest thing I ever done."

Hester was teaching her night class at the university. She telephoned a little after ten for a ride home. Rain was falling. I went from our house to the car under the cover of a black umbrella. I collapsed the umbrella and lay it on the back seat.

The rain was coming so fast and hard as I drove along I-20 into downtown, the wiper blades were not very effective. I was bent over the steering wheel, eyes close to the glass, trying to keep the car between painted lane markers, when I saw ten or twenty yards out ahead of me—or thought I saw—Is there a difference?—the hulking black shadow of a stalled car without lights. A collision was imminent. I slammed my foot against the brake pedal without the slightest idea what I hoped to accomplish by such means. The Honda went into a slide on the wet pavement. I relinquished control of the car and my life to the gods, steeling myself for the inevitable collision.

It did not happen. The car, going about its own business, righted itself neatly in the lane next to the one in which I had been driving, and continued its forward motion. I accelerated back to a safe speed, then glanced into the rearview mirror, hoping for a look at the stalled vehicle. But the instant I did this, the black umbrella in the back seat unfolded itself, obstructing my view to the rear. By the time I had reached into the back seat and shoved the umbrella aside, the scene behind me had vanished in darkness and rain.

I was sitting on the side porch of our house later that night ruminating on my freeway adventure when New York Doll called to me from the yard below the porch. "Mr. Author, come out here a minute."

I opened the front door of the house as Doll came up our porch steps. She still wore the plastic cup over her eye, but walked now without a crutch.

"You know that money I owe you?" she said.

"Nine dollars."

"Four."

"Nine," I insisted. "Those coins you gave me are worthless. Nobody will take them."

"You can trade them in for new at the Federal Reserve Bank. Give me a lift down to Englewood, I'll get you what I owe you. Guy down there owes me."

Englewood, a federal project housing, was black folks' turf. Police had found there recently a prison escapee who had gunned down half a dozen people in Chicago .

"You'll be all right, with me along," said Doll, reading my mind.

I told Hester where I was going. Did she want to come along?

"No, somebody should be here to collect the death benefit."

Doll and I drove south along Boulevard. Rain was falling again. I described what had happened to me on the freeway earlier that night.

"Somebody playin' with your mind," Doll said.

This was not impossible.

No one in the streets at Englewood, owing to the rain. We drove past rows of identical two-story brick apartment buildings.

"Park over there along the curb," Doll said. "I'll be right back."

She left the car. I locked both doors and sat, with the motor running, clutch depressed, and the car in gear, in case a getaway should be necessary. It was some time before she returned.

"We had an argument," she said, "I couldn't get any money. Have to pay y'all later... Thanks for the ride. Give my love to Hester."

Cheap taxi.

I never did hear from Pastor Ivey at the AME Church. But during the next week, the "heh-lo" lady telephoned repeatedly, and I received numerous times a recorded message: "You are cordially invited to attend the annual Christmas party of the Southside High School P.T.A. on Friday, December 18 at 7:30 P.M. in the school gymnasium. Entertainment will be provided by the mixed chorus and the concert band. Bring canned goods for distribution to the needy during the holidays."

The point was, I gathered, that as far as the African Methodist Episcopalians were concerned, being looted repeatedly by their own kind was preferable to stopping it with white assistance.

In my study late one night, I turned on the radio just as the announcer on one of Atlanta's classical music radio stations introduced a nocturne by Chopin. A little night music would be a fine thing, I thought. I sat down to listen.

The nocturne opened as sweetly as "Clair de Lune," but Chopin, who knew a thing or two about night, wasn't going to lie about it. The sweetness had given way to an eerie dissonance reminiscent for me of anxiety attacks at four and five A.M.—when a fist started pounding on the back door of the house adjacent to my study. The pounding fell like machine-gun fire on my sensibility honed to razor-sharpness by Chopin. Terrified and blinking, I hesitated before moving in my chair. Curiosity prevailing over caution, I turned off the radio and walked to the door.

"Who's there?" I asked in my deepest, most authoritative baritone.

"Satan come to punish you for yo sins," said an exaggeratedly deep black man's voice parodying mine. It was Mike. I opened the door.

He was shirtless and grinning. Thick through the chest and biceps, he looked like a middleweight fighter gone to seed.

"I thought it was the Boogie Man, and here it's just a fallen archangel!"

He flapped his arm-wings gracefully. "Yeah, I was flyin' over your house on my way back to Hell, and seen your light."

"Where's your shirt, Satan?"

"I lost my shirt."

"In a crap game?"

"A guy up to the rooming house took it."

"First your hair, now your shirt."

"Yeah. Gonna have to padlock my pecker, so nobody takes that... Come to tell you about my suicide attempt, if ain't too late."

It was late. But given the demands of his habit, I suspected that if I were to hear his story, it would have to be at his convenience, not mine. "Meet me at the front of the house," I said.

I gathered up writing materials and located an old V-neck sweater of mine (which, if Hester had had her way would have been long gone) and went to the front of the house. I let Mike in the front door, and we entered the screened side porch of the house where there was a table lamp.

I tossed him the sweater. "It isn't all that warm tonight.

"No, it ain't."

"I don't want you freezing up on me."

The sweater was too small for him. He exaggerated the difficulty of getting into it, then stared with comic dismay at his bellybutton protruding from underneath. "Sexy," he said.

"Very."

"So tell me your story."

"Could you advance me five?"

"Look, Satan, I've already advanced you five."

"Yeah, but that's gone."

I laughed. "You're going to have to perform for me a little before you get another advance."

"Yes, massa," he said.

He lit a cigarette and slung an elbow over the back of the porch swing. "Chapter one, Michael's suicide attempt."

He had been doing routine maintenance on a small fleet of pickup trucks owned by an old school friend, John Reed, and John was letting him drive one of the trucks home at night to Tyrone's rooming house.

Coming home Friday night, Mike was in good spirits. He would be paid for the work he had been doing next Wednesday, and then he would have his rent money for the month, and some left over. He had food and weed enough for the next few days. Susie Q., his woman at the time, was due back today from her grandmother's funeral in Macon. Good thing, too, because every woman he passed in the street that day, regardless of race, age or appearance, had looked to him like a basket of dead-ripe peaches.

In each of his two marriages, he had fallen prey to an unscrupulous woman who took him for all he had, so he had no inclination to marry again. But he liked Susie a lot. He wanted their relationship to continue.

He parked the pickup in front of the rooming house and went inside. In the front room at Tyrone's, there was a television set, two tattered armchairs, and a scattering of wooden folding chairs with "James Funeral Home" stenciled on the back slats. A corridor led from that room down the center of the house to the back. Tenants' rooms on either side of the corridor.

When Mike opened the door to his room, he saw Susie Q.'s loafers side-by-side under his bed, so she was back from Macon. He shoved his carpetbag full of tools under the bed, then stepped back into the corridor. Tyrone's door across the hall opened. Tyrone, who had a crack rock in one hand, seemed surprised to see him.

"Where Susie?" Mike asked.

"Ain't seen her," Tyrone said, and made his way swiftly down the corridor.

A room without a tenant for months had become a sort of clubroom. The roomers gathered there to drink, smoke, and watch television. The door—never locked—*was* now. None of the tenants had a key, so the door could only have been locked from inside. Mike knocked at the door. There was no response.

He walked to the rear of the house down a short flight of steps to the garden Susie had been tending that summer. Beyond the garden lay the steel shed, home of Chico and the German shepherd. He walked alongside the house back toward the street. Reaching the club room window, which had no blind, he saw Damon, who supplied Tyrone cocaine, lying on his tailbone in an armchair with his pants down and his long, thin arms dangling over the armrests to the floor. Susie Q. knelt between his legs, her Afro haircut bobbing as she polished the doorknob.

Bitch do anything for drugs, Mike thought, striding out to Jackson Street. He got into John Reed's truck and slammed the door. Driving south on Sycamore, he revved the motor so high, and shifted from first to second gear so fiercely, the clutch gave off a burning smell. He ran the stop sign at Sycamore and Pickett, nearly colliding with a car coming the other way, and headed over to Carver Homes, the federal housing project where he had grown up.

Standing on the same corner in Carver where he had been

on Friday and Saturday nights for twenty years was Leon Doby, friend of those in need.

Mike brought the truck to a halt beside Leon. Reaching across the cab, he rolled down the passenger-side window. Leon stuck his head into the cab. "Hey, bro, what's happenin'?"

The two men knocked knuckles.

"Leon, where can I find me a nice chick?"

"When you gotta have one, you gotta have one," said Leon, borrowing a line from a local hamburger chain's television commercials. "My man, you come to the right place. I know a lonely lady with fine titties on her, name Yvonne."

"This ain't some old beat-up used car?"

"No, man, this here's fine. Live by herself… I can deliver the goods fo the low, low price of fifty dollars, plus some weed for the lady."

"I got a problem, Leon. Broke til Wednesday."

"Yeah, you gotta problem," Leon agreed. But he thought about it. "That your truck?"

"No, workin' on it for a guy."

"He need it tomorrow?"

"Monday."

"Hock it."

"Hock it?"

"This guy I know–Marco–he give you a hundred for it tonight. You give him one-fifty tomorrow, get the truck back."

"High rate of interest," Mike observed.

"How bad you want pussy?"

"Where we go?"

Leon got into the truck. The two men drove a few blocks from Carver Homes down an alley behind a strip of business places, to a garage whose heavy wooden sliding doors stood open. There, a German shepherd, tail swishing, tongue hanging from its mouth in the heat, came from the garage to meet the two men.

A stubby, grizzle-haired black man with thick glasses and a grease-stained blue Atlanta Braves baseball cap, worked under a lift, wrench in hand.

Leon and Mike approached the lift.

"Hey, Pops, howya doin'?... Workin' late tonight, I see."

Marco noted their presence over one shoulder, seemingly without interest, and continued working. Leon explained why they had come.

The old man sprayed Nut-Buster on a frozen joint. Waiting for the solvent to work its magic, he wiped his hands on a red shop rag and contemplated the truck in the alley. "You got a title for this truck?" he asked Mike.

"In the glove compartment."

"You sign the truck over to me, and I'll loan you a hundred."

"Ain't my truck," Mike said.

"Yeah, I know that," Marco said, "but it ain't mine, neither. Somebody get in trouble for this, it ain't gonna be me, you hear what I'm sayin'?"

Mike nodded.

"You sign it in pencil, erase it later. Cost you one-fifty to get the truck back tomorrow, two hundred Sunday. Price goes up fifty a day."

Mike hesitated.

"I'll go call Yvonne," said Leon. He dialed a number on an old-fashioned rotary phone on the mechanic's desk in a corner of the garage. "If big titties don't scare you, Michael, you're gonna be a happy man tonight. Woman got titties outta this world."

Mike forged John Reed's signature in pencil, gave the title to Marco, and received in exchange five twenties. Leon was still on the phone, so Mike, accompanied by the German shepherd, wandered about the garage looking at the old man's setup.

"I repair cars myself," Mike said.

"That so?" said Marco.

"Worked on a fleet of trucks all this week, but don't get paid to Wednesday."

"That truck one of them?" Marco asked.

"Yeah."

Partitions in a back corner of the garage formed a small room. Mike peered through the doorway. There were crude wooden shelves without contents along one wall, and dog turds spread evenly over the concrete floor.

"Why all the poop in here, none out there?" Mike asked Marco.

"That's his room," Marco said. "If he does it out here, he knows I shoot him."

"Good arrangement," Mike said.

"All set," Leon said, "les go."

The two men set off on foot, stopping en route to Yvonne's at the house of one of Leon's business associates to buy joints. In a neighborhood of small frame houses, Leon nudged Mike down an alley. "We go in the back door so nobody snitches to Willy."

"Willy?"

"Her ex. Crazy Willy, they call him... jealous nigger."

They entered the backyard of a small house. "You wait

here," Leon said. Leon entered the back of the house.

Mike leaned back against the bough of a large weeping willow. A full moon shone through the willow branches. Full moon, Mike thought, and all the crazies be out: the fire bugs, the exhibitionists, the guy that hocked a truck for a hundred dollars who doesn't know where he'll come up with one-fifty tomorrow to get it back. He'd already spent most of what he had borrowed, but he was going to be very tight with what remained, to have a head start tomorrow in coming up with the one-fifty.

"Mike!" a woman's excited woman's voice said. "Let me in!"

I looked up from the notes I was making. Sparkle Plenty was on my front porch peering around a corner of the house at us on the side porch. Mike and I got to our feet. As I opened the front door of the house, Sparkle, breathing hard, leapt inside. She was wearing her cheerleader getup.

The squarish figure of Mzz Homer was silhouetted in the light of the doorway across the street.

"Mike, we gotta talk private," she said.

To give them time alone, I went to the kitchen, popped the tab on a can of beer, and poured the contents into a glass. Keats was right: Beaded bubbles do "blink" on the brim.

Hester came from the bedroom in her nightgown, eyes nearly shut, arms raised in front of her self-protectively like a sleepwalker's.

"Water," she said.

I pointed to the refrigerator.

"Someone in the house?"

"No one to speak of."

That seemed to quench her thirst, because she pivoted

and returned to the bedroom.

I drank a little of the beer. Glass in hand, I went up to the front of the house.

"Gotta little problem to clear up," Mike said. "We'll go on with the story later. Could you advance me five?"

Had I gotten my first five's worth? Might Sparkle's appearance have been prearranged to shorten our session, thereby increasing the number of fives Mike could extract from me later? No, that was paranoid. I advanced him five. Mike stepped out the door onto the front porch.

Sparkle, hand on the doorknob, lingered in the doorway a moment gazing about the living room. "Nice place," she said.

"Thanks."

"You're married, aren't you?"

"Yes."

She contemplated my crotch. "Pity."

New York Doll stuck her head into the doorway. "Hey! Could I have a cold one?" I handed her what was left of my glass of beer.

Mike peered back inside over Doll's head. "Meant to ask if I could borrow your lawnmower. Blade broke on ours up to the house, and the grass is gettin' real long."

"Anyone else need anything?" I said.

My remark caught Doll in mid-quaff. Laughing, she dribbled beer down the front of her blouse.

I removed the mower from the crawl space at the back of the house, and handed it over to Mike. The three of them went up the hill together, the plastic mower wheels clickety-clacking on the pavement.

The circumstances of life in the 'hood that summer had activated in me a capacity I had not known I possessed. In bed asleep, I could monitor the auditory environment at night, making subtle discriminations between innocuous sounds—a helicopter or an airliner passing overhead, the air conditioner condenser kicking in, my wife's snores resonating in the mattress coils—and other, suspicious ones.

In this state of slumberous sentience I heard that night over the air conditioner's steady hum emergency sirens winding down somewhere nearby, and then the sounds of big motors idling. A man's voice boomed from speakers, or perhaps a bullhorn. Sounds less remarkable had driven me wide-eyed from bed at three and four in the morning to peer out around the edge of curtains to the street. But whatever the situation in the street might have been, the authorities seemed to have it under control, and maybe that was why I did not get out of bed.

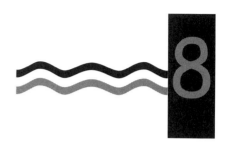

THE SURPRISED LOOK ON THE FURRY-FACED RAT in my garden path resembled so closely that of a guilty human being, I believed briefly in metempsychosis. The rat, up late that morning, skulked away.

I hoed weeds on a bright, cloudless summer morning. Squirrels played tag through the branches of the great oaks in the back lots. A blue jay came in for a perfect two point landing on a tomato stake, wobbling it. A hummingbird hovered trustingly inches from my face to see what it could see, before going on about its airy business. A ghostly-pale airliner, inaudible at its altitude, slipped effortlessly across the dome of my house, the backdrop to my act.

Suddenly, toward noon, old cars were rushing into the neighborhood from every direction at once. Four in tandem arrived in front of a drug house on Oak Street visible through tree leaves from my garden. The drivers and their riders left the cars, entered the house. It was, I realized, the fifteenth of July. The bi-monthly shrimp boat had arrived just as people had something to trade for drugs.

Shark, Tom Payne, and New York Doll, the three accused—by one another—of having stolen my fern, walked down Oak street chattering and laughing together. They, too, entered the drug house.

A little later, Tyrone came along the alley below my garden, all slicked-up in an archaic double-breasted gray suit, a broad tie with a garish pattern in which blue and orange predominated, and a straw-colored Panama hat. His cane struck a dandyish note. Seeing me, the guy who had beaten up New York Doll waved a greeting hand and lurched up a garden path to lay on me a glad hand and a black brother hug sweet with aftershave.

I felt a revulsion in his physical presence. Had it been in my power at that moment to deport him and this entire tribe of degenerates to some equivalent of Siberia, I would have done so.

"Wilson found your saw," I said, glad for an excuse to retreat from him to the crawl space of my house where I had stored the saw.

"Well, there's my old friend after all these years!" he gushed, as I handed him the saw.

He seemed to sense my hostility. He was soon on his way down the alley.

A rental truck of the kind used commonly by the drug boys to move merchandise around the city pulled up across the street from the house on Oak Street that was attracting the crowd. The driver turned off the motor. I looked at the two men in the cab, they looked at me. They were looking at me, probably, as I went up the back steps to my house and through the door to place a call to the police.

I got Captain Turnipseed on the line and described the scene on Oak Street. He said he would send an officer to investigate.

The men in the truck watched me descend my back steps, pick up my hoe, and resume work.

A squad car turned up Oak Street from Jackson and parked nose-to-nose with the rental truck. A man in the passenger's seat of the truck leaned out the window. "Hey, cop dude! What's happenin', Dave?"

The driver got out of the truck, threw his hands into the air, and bugged out his eyes. "Don't shoot! We give up, don't shoot!"

Smiling Dave, a roly-poly young black cop, was grinning as he ambled toward the truck, holster rolling on the wave of fat at his hip.

I concentrated on the weeds.

When I glanced over toward Oak Street again, all three men were looking in my direction and smiling. Shortly after that, both the truck and squad car vanished.

I was in the house at lunch when Turnipseed called to say that Officer Harris had determined the men in the truck were moving furniture for an elderly woman who lived on Oak Street. There was no elderly woman living on Oak Street.

On my front porch, I resumed reading of Juvenal's "Against the City of Rome."

Shut up your house or your store,
Bolts and padlocks and bars will never keep out all the
*   burglars,*
Or a holdup man will do you in with a switchblade.
If the guards are strong over Pontine marshes and

pinewoods
Near Volturno, the scum of the swamps and filth of
   the forest
Swirl into Rome, the great sewer, their sanctuary, their
   haven.
Furnaces blast and anvils groan with the chains we are
   forging:
What other use have we for iron and steel? There is
   danger
We will have little left for hoes and mattocks and
   ploughshares.
Happy the men of old, those primitive generations
Under the tribunes and kings, when Rome had only
   one jailhouse!

"The neighborhood's been busy today," Wilson called to
me from his porch.

I looked up from the page. "Yeah, it's the fifteenth of the
month."

"What was that ruckus out in the street late last night?"

"I was going to ask you."

"It was uphill somewhere."

A solidly-built, compact, young black man came up the
hill on Jackson with a tall aluminum stepladder balanced on
his shoulders. "Ladder for sale—just forty dollars!"

I recognized the big splotch of brown paint on the side
panel of the ladder Tyrone had sold me for twelve dollars.

"Where'd you steal it?" I inquired.

"My uncle died and left it to me," he said, but did not
linger to continue his pitch.

"A person wouldn't want to be an uncle," I said to
Wilson. "So many of them die."

"You're telling this to a school teacher?" Wilson said. "Was that your ladder?"

"Used to be."

"We could have jumped him."

"I wasn't in the mood." Besides, the ladder was doing its part in the redistribution of the national wealth.

The phone rang. I went into the house.

"Is your number— ——?" a black woman's voice inquired.

"Yes."

"I receive a letter from Bell South say your phone is gonna be disconnect cause you ain't paid yo bill."

"But I have paid my bill."

"I dunno, that's what it says."

"Why would you get such a letter?"

This turning of the tables produced a hesitation at the other end of the line. "I really couldn't say."

"What's your number?"

"This is a pay phone." She hung up.

Mischief.

But just to be sure, I called Southern Bell. No, there was nothing in their records to suggest that my account was in arrears.

I went back to Juvenal.

I was getting out of my chair to get myself a drink of water when I noticed a pair of skinny-shanked black boys in droopy-drawer shorts coming up the hill. One had a beer bottle in his hand. I had just stepped into the house when I heard glass breaking on the pavement. I turned around. Shards of wet sepia-colored glass glinted on the sunny pavement. The boys were continuing on their way up the hill. I was furious.

"Hey! What is this?" I shouted after them.

The two swung around to face me. I braced for a smart-ass retort—but there was none.

"I told you," the one boy said to the other.

"Let's clean it up!" I commanded.

The boy who was evidently the guilty party trudged back downhill to the broken glass, looked at it, and then up at me: *Clean it up with what?* Had I not been so angry, I might have offered him a broom and dustpan.

He knelt on my front walk picking up the pieces of broken glass with one hand, and placing them delicately in the palm of the other. I recognized him now as one of that ragtag clan from the tumbledown bungalow up around the corner on Sycamore. Maggie Spitz had told me how the boy's mother, a crack addict and prostitute, had disappeared last spring, leaving a half dozen children in her mother's care. Shortly after that, the grandmother had had a stroke. She had been at Grady Hospital ever since, leaving the children to shift for themselves. An uncle came by with food occasionally. Concerned neighbors, black and white, were helping out as they could. After the city cut off water to the house, the children drew drinking water, and water to flush the commode, from neighbors' garden-hoses. One day Maggie had run the children, one after the other, through her shower, and washed their clothes in her machine. Rats drawn by the delectable odors of garbage and excrement had been excavating around the foundation posts at night, looking for ways in.

The boy now rose to his feet and looked around for a place to deposit his collection of broken glass.

"Put it in there," I said, pointing to Wilson's trash receptacle standing at curbside for the sanitation crew. The boy did so, then started back up the hill to rejoin his friend. He was examining his hand. Then they both examined it.

"Do it hurt?"

The boy nodded that it did.

Evidently he had cut his hand on the glass. Now of a mind to temper justice with mercy, I asked if the boy if he wanted a Band-Aid.

They looked at me uncomprehendingly.

"You need a bandage for your hand?"

I didn't think they grasped my meaning, but they seemed to have decided I meant no harm, because they came up the walk to my porch.

"Be right back," I said, going into the house for a Band-Aid and hydrogen peroxide. They were on the porch when I returned outside. Cute kids actually, younger than I had thought, maybe eleven or twelve.

"Let me see that hand," I said. The boy laid his right hand, palm up, in mine. It was weighty there: the outsized puppy paw prefiguring the big dog to come. I looked for the cut, but there wasn't any.

The second boy pointed to meaty flesh below the thumb. "Bee sting him."

Yes, I could see the swelling. "You dropped the bottle when the bee stung you?"

The boy nodded in the affirmative. "He was in the bottle."

So the boy had been remiss only in walking away from the mess he had created unintentionally. His sore hand made that understandable.

"I thought you'd cut your hand on the glass," I explained. "I'm afraid the Band-Aid won't do much for a bee sting."

The second boy nodded agreement. "Won't do no good."

But the boy who had been stung took the Band-Aid from my open hand and slipped it into the breast pocket of his T-shirt before the two left my porch and continued on their way. The Band-Air was a gift from an adult, and there had not been many of those that long hot summer.

I felt I needed to get away for a while.

I got into my car and drove up the hill from Jackson to Boulevard. A red light there stopped me. Bill Clinton sat at the window of his new home.

Across the street, the two homeless men were once again at the entrance to the split-level house. "Son of a bitch," declared the one, trying to swat with a rolled-up newspaper the wasp circling his head.

I drove up I-20 to I-75, and headed south on 75 out of Atlanta without any destination in mind. Beyond the city, I steered the car off the freeway into country roads that would take me back where I belong, and had been driving for an hour when I came upon a second-hand store at a rural crossroads.

I was an aficionado of second-hand stores and pawnshops because of my loyalty to the electric-mechnical typewriters manufactured by Smith-Corona in the 1960s and 1970s. I had used these machines for years in my work. They had been obsolete a long time, but I still found them in good condition in second-hand stores. Because of their age, they broke down pretty frequently. Repair labor was expensive, and parts hard to find, so when one failed me, I just trashed it and started using another I had picked up somewhere for ten or fifteen dollars. Being always in the market for old typewriters was not exactly the Grail quest, but it had some of that quest's alluring indefiniteness and renewability.

I parked the car in front of the store. A crude sign on the door announced a "One Day Sale" on vinyl records and tapes. The regular price, a dollar, had been "slashed in half."

There were no typewriters, but I knelt in a corner of the store among pasteboard boxes filled with long-playing records and cassettes. East European peasants in native dress cavorted gaily on the faded cover of a collection of dances by Liszt, Chopin, and Dvorak; and I found two other long-playing records to my liking.

The portly fellow with the mustache at the antique cash register resembled physically Oliver Hardy (a native Georgian). He wore red suspenders and an Alpine cap with a peacock feather in the brim. He tried to charge me a dollar each for the three items I had chosen.

"I thought tapes and records were half-price."

"That was yesterday."

"That's not what your sign says."

"What sign?"

I pointed to the door.

He glanced that way, and sighed in disgust. "I told Don to take down that sign this morning… If you want something done right, do it yourself."

He went to the door, opened it, and reached around its edge to tear away the sign. As he did so, the feather in his cap brushed the door jamb, and the cap fell to the floor. He picked up the hat, brushed it off a little, and put it back on his head. Using the door glass as a mirror, he adjusted the hat to a jaunty angle on his head, and rejoined me at the cash register.

"I'll give you the Friday price," he said.

"Otherwise I could sue for false advertising," I said gravely.

He smiled at my irony, but then fixed me with a serious look. "Three for one-fifty is a very good deal."

"Of course," I said, "a lot of people don't even have turntables any more."

"They don't know what they're missing," he said.

I got back in my car and drove on in the same way I had been going. A short distance down the road, there was a simple rectangular white sign with black letters on a stake at roadside.

GRIFFIN 6

A classic American small town! Not some little Roman village, maybe, but close enough. I would go to Griffin.

I parked the car on a side street in downtown Griffin and walked a block to the Victorian-American Main Street lined with two and three story commercial buildings. Stark light of a blazing July sun bleached buildings facing west on the far side of the street. It was light by Edward Hopper.

The streets were empty, but this was not surprising; I remembered how the Main Street of my Ohio hometown used to empty out on hot midsummer afternoons. But as I walked along Main Street, I saw how many store and office fronts were boarded over with sheet plywood.

Two cops stood on one corner. I nodded a greeting to them as I passed. They stared icily at me. Down the street a bit further, I turned to look back at them, and they were still watching me. I was a suspicious case.

At the end of the commercial district in the direction I walked was an A&P supermarket open for business! There had been and A&P on the Main Street of my home town! I had not been in an A&P for years.

I went inside. A big sign over the checkout advertised a sale on "Eight o' Clock" coffee. Eight o' Clock coffee! My mother used to buy the stuff at A&P in the 1940s! I located the coffee display. The coffee was still sold in bean form, and there was a sturdy red steel coffee grinder, a dead-ringer for the one at the A&P in my hometown. The sale price was excellent. I picked up three bags of "Eight o'Clock," opened the sacks, and started running their contents through the grinder.

To a young black man stocking shelves nearby, I said, "You know, A&P's house coffee was called Eight o' Clock back in the 1940s."

He glanced up from his work and took stock of garrulous old me.

"The A&P in my hometown in Ohio had a coffee grinder that looked exactly like this one."

"If it ain't broke," he said, "don't fix it."

Carrying my purchases in a plastic bag, I crossed Main Street and went back the way I had come. Vacant stores and offices on that side of the street, too, and the window displays of surviving businesses were perfunctory, as if no one really expected window-shoppers.

Turning down a side street, I walked past what had once been the town movie theater, now closed. Some joker had installed posters for *Gone with the Wind* in the showcases on either side of the ticket booth. This was what was left of a classic American downtown after the major corporations were done with it.

I had seen as much of Griffin as I cared to see, and was opening my car door, when at my back I heard the roar of old car motors, and sounds of bass music—*Dada, DOOOM!… Dada DOOOOOM!…Dada DOOOOOM!*

A slow parade of wide, lowslung 1980s cars, each driven by a young man with a baseball cap turned backward down his neck, passed by me. I thought I knew what their business was.

A medium-sized U-Haul truck stood in the driveway of the rap musicians' house, 533 Jackson, as I arrived back home.

There did not seem to be much point in calling Turnipseed to tell him drugs were probably being delivered across the street. I stood in my living room gazing through my binoculars as two of the renters carried a sofa (packed with cocaine?) into the truck. A huge, blurry Kevin crossed my line of vision. I went to the door and opened up before he could knock.

"Where were you today?" Kevin asked.

"Out of town."

He sat down on the porch railing. He had the little finger of one hand in his mouth and was gnawing fiercely at a hangnail. There were bloody cuticles on other fingers of that hand.

"Whatcha think about what happened?"

"I don't know. What happened?"

"Terry."

"Terry?"

My ignorance of the local characters and events that constituted for him the whole of reality surprised and amused him, ordinarily, but now he seemed exasperated by it. "That fat boy with thick glasses, run with the drug boys on Oak?"

"I think I know the one you mean. What about him?"

"He killed hisself up to Tyrone's last night."

I stared at him.

"You didn't hear the noise? There was EMS and cop cars and television stations…"

"What happened?"

"Bunch of us was sitting around Tyrone's smokin' with the whores. We was high. Tyrone said, 'Let's play Russian roulette.' Sparkle Plenty said, don't, but he went and got his gun. Couple guys pull the trigger, nothing happen. They give it to Terry."

Kevin slid down the railing, distancing himself further from me in the doorway.

"Terry was about here, I was where you are." He put his forefinger to his temple. "Pow!" He continued sitting upright on the railing several seconds, staring at me with a dead man's fixity, then tumbled from the railing, hitting the floor with bruising force. He lay motionless there, eyes gazing up at me glassily. It was a convincing performance; I was trembling again, and my mouth was bone dry.

Kevin got back to his feet, sat on the railing again, and put his hand back into his mouth. His eyes were opaque, the focus of his attention inward. He gnawed at the hangnail.

He remembered something else: "Weren't no blood at all 'til the coroner come and turned him over. Then it started pourin' outta him… Terry's uncle thinks Tyrone and me set him up."

"Did you?"

"Not me… Tyrone and him argued about money."

"Drug money?"

He nodded yes.

Abandoning my porch abruptly, he went off down Jackson toward Confederate.

I telephoned Maggie. "I just heard about Terry."

"Where were y'all last night?"

"Slept right through it. We had the air conditioner going."

"It was a circus out in the street."

"So I hear. The family thinks Kevin set up Terry?"

"Yeah. Terry's uncle has been driving around and around Kevin's parents' house all day. Kevin's scared shitless."

"Did he have anything to do with it?"

"Well, he was talkin' real crazy when the cops arrived last night. I told him he better shut his damn mouth…. Did you hear the rap musicians were evicted?"

"I saw the rental van out front, I didn't know they were evicted."

"They're history. Landlord got sick of 'em tearing up the place."

The evicted tenants continued to pack household goods into the truck through the early evening. About ten, the truck and the rappers' cars drove off. That, it seemed, was that.

Hester went to bed before me that night. I sat on the side porch of our house listening to midsummer crickets jangling, wondering what the guy in the second-hand store had meant that afternoon when he said, "They don't know what they're missing."

John the Drunk was involved in some kind of altercation with two Alaskan huskies behind a chainlink fence at the foot of the hill.

Woofwoofwoofwoofwoofwoofwoofwoofwoof!

"Well, woof-woof-woof to you, too, you blue-eyed sons o' bitches!"

"**K**NEW I SHOULDN'T DONE IT when I done it," Mike said. "I left your mower out back the house last night, and a guy stole it. I know who it was, Mzz Tanner seen him with it. Call 911, and we go get it back."

I had intended to continue reading Juvenal that morning, but I called 911.

Mike and I sat on the front steps of my house waiting for a patrolman.

"Gotta cold one?"

"You lose my mower, and you have the gall to ask me for a beer?"

Tyrone's new roomer, Billy, came down the hill. He smiled ingratiatingly. "Sir, I need to go to McDonald's for sumpin to eat. Could I borrow your car?"

"No."

I turned to Mike. "Was somebody chasing Sparkle Plenty when she came here the other night?"

"Yeah. That old guy she stays with in Cabbagetown. He thought she was messin' around with some dude."

"Doesn't that kind of go with the territory, if you live

with a prostitute?"

"He was real mad."

"How old is this old guy?"

"About fifty. She likes older guys.... I think she kind of likes you."

"You out pimping today, Satan?"

His green eyes (legacy of the Irishman who had crept into the family tree, he'd once told me) twinkled. Getting me involved with one of their women would no doubt be a fine way to assure my loyalty.

A squad car driven by a white officer pulled to the curb in front of my house.

Mike told the officer what had happened. The three of us got into the squad car, Mike and I in the rear behind the protective grill. The officer, following Mike's instructions, drove to an address north on Sycamore where an addict, Red Ransom, lived with his mother.

"You want to press charges if he has the mower?" the officer asked me as we walked toward the house.

"I just want my mower back."

Red Ransom's mother came to the door.

"I don't know where he is, officer. If you find him, lock him up. He steals from me just like everybody else."

"I notice you have a garage, ma'am," the officer said. "OK if we look back there?"

"Go right ahead."

Red was asleep in the back seat of his mother's car. The officer dragged him out of the car and confronted him with the information Mzz Tanner supplied about the theft of my mower. Red agreed to show us where the mower was when he heard I would not press charges.

"See ya later," Mike said, heading down Sycamore toward Tyrone's. I was obviously on my own now.

The officer searched Red for weapons, then put him in the back of the squad car. I sat in the front seat under a rifle rack. Red supplied directions. We drove through the narrow early twentieth-century residential back streets on the west side of Grant Park, and up a driveway between a bungalow and a vacant lot. Under a towering Southern pine at the front of the vacant lot, a salt- and pepper-haired black man sat on an antique church pew surrounded by urns, bird baths, and pink lawn herons that were evidently for sale.

"Where's the mower?" the officer asked Red, who pointed to a weathered-gray wooden shed leaning to one side at the back of the vacant lot. I described my mower to the officer.

"How do," said the cop, walking past the man seated on the pew, who did not appear to have seen anyone walk past him.

Sounds of furniture being moved in the shed.

I got out of the squad car, leaned back against the front fender, and folded my arms across my chest. The man on the pew stared hard at me.

"Yo," I said.

The officer came from the shed pushing a red mower. The man on the pew did not appear to have seen a man pushing a red mower pass by him.

"That it?" the cop said.

"I recognize the scratched paint on the front."

The officer turned to the man on the pew. "You know, if this man wanted to press charges, both of you would be going downtown with me."

The man on the pew might have been a lawn ornament.

A cable had been disengaged from a lever on the mower's motor housing. As the officer knelt to reattach the cable, the man on the pew rose and walked to the squad car. He bent forward and looked into the open window at Red Ransom.

"Mmmmm-MHM!" he said.

Then he walked back to the pew and sat down.

In front of my house, the officer and I had just lifted the mower out of the trunk of the squad car when I noticed Corinne Boardman's lifelong friend, Mattie, in the yard between Mzz Boardman's house and mine. She was looking up toward Mzz Boardman's windows and calling, "Corinne? … Corinne?"

"What's wrong, Mattie?"

"Oh, I've been trying to reach her by phone all morning, and she doesn't answer. I'm afraid something's wrong. You have a copy of her door key, don't you?"

"Yes."

"Would you get it and let me in?"

I located the key, and Mattie and I walked onto Mzz Boardman's porch.

"Lord only knows what we'll find in there," Mattie said.

I rang the doorbell.

"Corinne?!" Mattie called.

"Has she been ill?"

"Has she been well?" Mattie said. "She was a sickly teenager. Sickly in middle-age. She hasn't improved at eighty-two. Her lungs don't work, she has kidney problems, poor circulation, arthritis, I don't know what-all. Never had any brains to start with."

"You've known her all your life?"

"We went to grammar school together.... Go ahead, use the key."

I did so. The door opened only a few inches. A night chain was in place.

"Corinne?" Mattie called.

"Well, if you weren't so impatient, Mattie, I'd have answered the phone," Mzz Boardman said from somewhere down near the floor. I put my shoulder into the door and tore the night chain out of the woodwork. Mzz Boardman, wearing a long flannel nightgown and her red boots, lay curled on her living room floor.

"Oh, Corinne, you've gone and hurt yourself, sure as anything!" Mattie cried.

"I just had a little fall. If you'd help me back into bed, so I can get my sleep..."

"Look at you, you're shivering, and you peed all over the floor, you naughty girl."

Mattie went off into a bedroom at the back of the house. I knelt beside Mzz Boardman.

"She never would listen to me," Mzz Boardman said.

Mattie returned with a blanket which she spread over her old friend. "I never listened to you because nothing you ever said made a lick of sense."

"Everything will be fine in the morning," Mzz Boardman said.

"It is morning, you goose!"

"If you could just help me into bed..."

"Corinne, we can't move you! You might have broken something!"

"I broke my hip when I fell in 1989, but I learned my lesson."

Mattie took me aside. "She's completely out of her head."

"How can you tell?"

"The garbage can lids froze tight in January," Mzz Boardman said. "Can you imagine?"

"We should call her nephew Joe," Mattie said.

"Don't you bother Joe," Mzz Boardman said. "He's busy writing his dissertation. He's going to be a doctor, you know, but not the kind that gives you pills."

"Dissertation pissertation," Mattie said. "Time he paid you a little attention, if you ask me."

"That fern in the bathroom hasn't been watered," Mzz Boardman said.

I found Joe Boardman's home and work phone numbers on a list of numbers taped to the woodwork beside the old rotary wall phone in the kitchen, and reached him at the suburban high school where he taught. He asked me to call the paramedics and have them take his aunt to Georgia Baptist Hospital. He would set out for Atlanta immediately.

The paramedics were a thick-set black woman, and a bald white man with a weightlifter's body and an earring.

"Howya doin', sweetie?" the man cooed, dropping his leather satchel of medical instruments to the wood floor.

"I'm fine."

"Well, honeybunch, you don't look so fine lyin' there on the floor... Pretty red boots."

"Thank you."

"What happened here?"

"Nothing," Mzz Boardman said with a touch of irritation in her voice. "I was going to the phone as fast as I could, but Mattie's so impatient."

"You hurt anywhere, darlin'?"

"No, I'm just resting. I'll get up and have my breakfast soon now."

"Do you think you broke any bones?"

The black woman was pressing Mzz Boardman's flesh lightly here and there. When she touched the right shoulder, Mzz Boardman flinched.

"I think she may have broken her collarbone," the black woman said.

"There's no need for this fuss," Mzz Boardman said.

"Would you let us take you over to Georgia Baptist for some nice X-rays," the male paramedic said.

"No."

"If I said please?"

"No.'

"Pretty please?"

"I'd just pick her up and haul her out of here, if I were you," Mattie said.

"M'am, we can get in all kinds of legal trouble doing that."

"With Corinne? You've got to be kidding."

The paramedics continued to attempt to gain Mzz Boardman's consent, but could not, and finally drove off leaving her lying on the floor.

When Joe Boardman reached Georgia Baptist Hospital and found his aunt had not been admitted, he drove to the house, scooped up Mzz Boardman in both arms, and whisked her off to the hospital in his red Toyota.

Hester was participating in a symposium in north Atlanta one night, and I was getting dinner for myself, when someone started banging a fist against a front window of my house—a method of announcing one's presence common in the 'hood that probably had rural origins, but could scare bejeezus out of a city-dweller.

Walking to the front of the house I was thinking how I was a rural-urban, Northern farmer's grandson whose devotion to truth and beauty had reduced him to a cross between housewife, handyman, and English country squire.

"Hey in there!" yelled a black woman.

"Hey out there!" I responded, as I opened the front door.

"Remember me—Betty? I got the money I owe you."

It was the woman I had thought stole my mail. She wore a shamrock-green silk jockey-style cap and a matching fitted blouse. The outfit evoked the indistinct memory of a fashionable look from the Sixties or Seventies. A trifle faded with age, the outfit was still jaunty enough.

Betty was smiling. "Told you I'd be back with your money."

"That was some time ago," I said.

"Better late than never!"

"Did you get the job?"

Her eyes slid to one side. "They gonna call me."

She held out a folded bill in the bunched fingertips of one hand. I opened my hand to receive it. Her fingertips went down on the sensitive flesh at the center of the palm and opened with a feathery lightness, releasing the five dollar bill.

"I only loaned you three-fifty, as I recall."

"Interest," she said.

"I don't charge interest." I opened my wallet and gave her

two bills.

"Smells good in there," she said.

"I'm cooking dinner."

"Ain't you gonna invite me, honey?" she said, laying a hand on my forearm.

"Got to go before things burn," I said, shutting the house door and locking it.

That wasn't interest, honey, that was an investment. The weird, conniving friendliness of these people—one strategy, among others, for extracting what they needed in order to live. Joel Chandler Harris said to me, "Remember my Uncle Remus stories? All those tales about that charming rogue Br'er Rabbit outwitting the more powerful Br'er Fox and Br'er Bear?" I did, yes. Harris had been an Atlantan, too.

Dining alone, I had the morning Constitution I had not read earlier in the day propped against salt and pepper shakers.

The paper published once a week a list of real estate transfers in various zipcode areas. That day's list included, I noticed, the sale of Mzz Kitchens' property on Jackson Avenue not to "Tamara Thompson" or "Tamika Thomas," but to "Tamara Tomasso"—the woman of many names.

Opening to the editorial pages, I found myself staring into the mirror of my own words: the op-ed piece I had written after the public safety meeting at the church back in the spring:

Mayor C., Deputy Police Chief R., Captain T., and an assortment of other Atlanta officials agreed to play scapegoats at a fangs-bared gathering of Grant Park neighbors, including me, the other night.

In our section of southeast Atlanta, surrounded by some of Atlanta's poorest neighborhoods, drug-related crime rates rise and fall. Lately, they have been up, especially for car thefts and break-ins. People are furious.

In a gripe session lasting two hours at St. Paul's Methodist Church, a sizable crowd voiced complaints about nearly every conceivable aspect of local police and judicial operations: inadequate patrolling of streets, early releases for convicted felons, the failure to prosecute people apprehended for crimes, police indolence, slow or non-existent 911 responses.

The officials who had agreed to show up—aware no doubt of what they were in for—maintained throughout the evening an almost otherworldly professional calm.

Their bureaucratic self-assurance and equanimity provoked increasingly inflammatory remarks from some of us tired of the usual police baloney. Nothing we said seemed to affect our imperturbable leaders, though. They promised humbly to do better in the future. There would be modifications of leadership, new strategies, hopefully more citizen "input."

Even while helping flog these long-suffering fellows, I was thinking: The real problems confronting us have scarcely anything to do with law enforcement, and a lot to do with poverty, and the increasingly urgent socioeconomic distresses of our urban underclass. The reason we were not talking about these was that their connection with our immediate, tangible distresses was abstract and indefinite.

And, in truth, which of us knew what to do about the underlying problems? What we were attacking instead of these problems were our police, in what amounted to scapegoating.

The police being associated as closely with the idea of public order as they are, the illusion arises that they might be able to wave big guns like wands and produce that order. A comforting thought, this; and the thought likely to follow is: Well, why haven't they?

Our illusions in these matters were obvious enough, no

doubt, to the canny cops at our meeting. The prestige of their calling rests largely on those very illusions, so they had not been eager to dispel them.

The meeting served as a reminder how, in societies which refuse, or do not know how, to deal with their most fundamental problems, police and/or dictators may acquire real power by promising solutions they cannot possibly deliver.

The mentality on display at St. Paul's that night seemed to me to have been precisely the one that begets police states; and I had been as much involved in it as the cops.

What a lot of wimpy nonsense! To hell with the socioeconomic origins of criminal behavior! I wanted law and order! Bring on the National Guard, if necessary! I would rather have to present identification every time I entered and left my neighborhood than endure the terrors of liberty. Lock up these degenerates in jails or mental institutions and throw away the damned keys!

I was on my front porch steps after dinner when Mike came down the hill.

"Hear you got your mower back."

"Yes."

"Sorry about that."

"All's well that ends well.... Been meaning to ask you, by the way, if you'd like to have my old Toyota."

"You're giving it away?"

"It's just standing in the yard collecting rust."

He dropped to his knees on the walk below the porch steps, extended his arms full-length in front of him, and salaamed repeatedly. "Thank you, massa, thank you."

"Don't do this to me, Mike," I said. "Look, it isn't that

big a deal. The car isn't running."

"You think I can nigger-rig it?"

"You refer, I think, to Afro-engineering?... There's something seriously wrong with the motor. Maybe you'll be able to get it going, maybe not. If not, you can sell it to a junkyard."

"You could do that."

"You need the money worse than I do."

"Sure, I'll take it off your hands."

There was an acrid, metallic smell in the air. The street light in front of our house had just come on, and a cloud of blue smoke had settled around it.

"What's that smell?"

"Shark's up to Tyrone's meltin' copper wire," Mike said.

"Melting copper wire?"

"Yeah. Guys get it outta lampposts on the freeway. Melt it down, you can sell it. You know that stretch of I-20 between Boulevard and Moreland where there ain't lights no more? That's why."

The redistribution of the national wealth happened in a money economy, one way or another.

"Wanna go on with my story?" Mike asked.

"Sure."

I went into the house for the notes I had made earlier, and writing materials, and rejoined Mike on the front porch steps.

"Let's see... When we left off, Leon and you had just arrived at Yvonne's house," I said.

Leon introduced Mike to Yvonne, a short, bosomy young woman with a pretty round face. Her red velvet sweater slipped off one shoulder intriguingly. The small living room *looked like* a whore house: big red flowers all over the sofa fabric and the drapes; tall, pink-tinted transparent glass end table lamps with tasseled gold fabric shades. There was an old-fashioned mantel with a big oval mirror over it.

"You're cute, honey," Yvonne said to Mike, slipping her arm around his waist. "Big strong man."

"I got the food, baby, if you got the plate," Mike said. "What we gonna do?"

Yvonne flapped a hand at him. "Listen to him, Leon! This man moves right along, don't he? Sit down, Mike, let's get acquainted, smoke some of that nice weed you got, get in the mood."

Mike felt he was already in the mood, and as a good a way as any for them to get acquainted would be for him to get out of the mood. But it took two to tango. He sat down in an armchair. Yvonne and Leon sat on the sofa across the room. It did not take three to tango.

They passed around joints. At first Yvonne was favoring Mike with pretty smiles, and peepshow leg-crossings, but she and Leon became engrossed in a discussion of the troubled marriage of mutual friends, and she seemed to have forgotten Mike was in the room.

Mike's thoughts wandered to the question of how he was going to come up with a hundred-fifty dollars tomorrow to get John Reed's truck out of hock.

"You know what I'd like?" Yvonne said, turning her attention back to him. "Some nice red wine—burgundy."

"Liquor store right around the corner," Leon said.

Mike and Leon walked to the liquor store. "This is a classy lady," Leon said. "Don't get no cheap shit."

The burgundy cost Mike most of another twenty.

On the way back to Yvonne's, Mike said, "Leon, when do I get to be alone with the chick?"

"I was just helping warm things up for y'all."

"Yeah, well, they're warm enough. Time for you to go home."

"Ain't no problem with that," Leon said, handing the bottle of wine to Mike and disappearing down an alley.

Should have done that a long time ago, Mike thought.

Yvonne had dozed off on the sofa with her legs tucked up under her prettily when he reentered the house through the back. He put down the wine bottle with a thud on the coffee table in front of her.

Her eyes opened. "Where's Leon?"

"He go home," Mike said. "Time for you and me to get it on, baby."

"You got the wine?"

"Yeah, but I don't want no wine, I want you!"

Yvonne stretched languorously and yawned. "What's the matter, honey, don't you think you're going to get your money's worth?"

"Well, it kind of seems like that, yeah!"

"Come here, sweetie." She reached out for his hand, and drew him down on the sofa beside her, slipped onto his lap, and crooked one arm around his neck. Her other hand became active.

He ran his hand up under the sweater.

"You like the way that feels?" she said.

"Yes, ma'am, I do."

"I drive you crazy before it's over and done with, Mikey .... Would you like that?"

"I would."

"What's that?" she said, looking toward a window across the room.

"What what?"

"That sound."

He hadn't heard anything.

She removed his hand from under her sweater, walked across a room, and peered around the edge of a window blind. "There it is again, like somebody scratchin' on a screen."

"You expecting company?"

"Crazy Willie come around sometimes late like this, when the light on."

"Turn out the light."

"Might make it worse if he think somebody's here."

The phone rang. Yvonne went into the kitchen to answer it. She closed a door behind her. Mike could hear her voice, but could not tell what she was saying. The clock on the mantel told the hour as nearly the beginning of the day Mike would have to come up with one hundred-fifty dollars to get John Reed's truck back.

Yvonne came out of the kitchen. "That was Delores across the street," she whispered. "Someone in the bushes out front of my house. Probably Willie... Honey, I'm too scared to do anything with him around. Will you take a raincheck?"

"Hey, you tryin' to get out of the deal?'

"Shhhh!... One time, he come around late at night like this and shoot out that window right behind your head."

Mike looked over his shoulder. The window framed his head perfectly.

"Bullet hit right here," Yvonne said, pointing to what indeed looked very much like a bullet-hole in the mantel. "I told Delores, I got this sweet boy over here, but I can't do nothing for him, cause I'm scared. She say, you send that sweet boy over here—I'll do him."

"I paid you!" Mike said. "You suppose to do me!"

"My hands is tied," Yvonne whispered.

"I wish to hell they was, I'd beat shit outta you!"

"Shhhh!"

A little door in the front of the mantel clock opened, and a plastic bird came forth, said, "cuckoo" twelve times in a thin, electronic voice, and returned back inside the clock.

Mike backhanded the wine bottle, which flew off the table and rolled across the room.

Mike rose from my porch steps. "End, part two."

"Is it just my imagination," I said, "or are these sessions of ours getting shorter?"

"When the creative power give out, she gone," Mike said. "Ain't nothing I can do about it. Think it's probably going to take another five to get her going again. One more time ought to about do it."

"If I advance you a five for the end of the story, you'll show up?"

"I gotta conscience."

I regretted now that, when promising him five dollars per session, I had not specified how long a session would last.

I advanced him five.

A FIRE AT GRANDMA MITCHELL'S bed-and-breakfast one afternoon burned through the front third of the house before firemen had it under control.

Given the character of the tenants that summer, the neighbors suspected arson. Mzz Grant claimed to have seen two strange men loitering near the house shortly before the fire started. But Channel Two's account of the fire on the evening news made it clear the house had not been "torched." A four-year-old boy imitating Grandma Mitchell's lighting a barbecue grill had poured lighter fluid across her porch floor and dropped a lighted match on it.

"Then what happened, Derrick?" inquired the cajoling, saccharine voice of Channel Two's female reporter. She thrust a microphone in front of pop-eyed young Derrick.

"Go poof!" he said, delighted obviously by the stupendous consequences of such a simple act.

The fire was being discussed as Jake Macht drove about the area picking up neighbors who would attend a meeting with a narcotics investigator lawyer Bill Avery on Lee Street had arranged for us.

"The firemen said they had trouble finding a hydrant that worked," Melinda Spack remarked.

"Oh, they always say that," Jake said, "but a lot of times they'll just let old houses burn. The city regards it as a form of slum clearance."

"Well, it was a blessing in disguise, if you ask me," Melinda said. "That situation was going from bad to worse."

The fire had indeed suggested the gods might be on the side of the insurgent middle class against the hapless natives.

"Now, if we could just get a good blaze going at Tyrone's house," Jake said.

"That might be possible," Maggie Spitz said from the rear of the van. "Kevin said the cops were up there this morning. Tyrone called them, because one of the roomers stole his gas can."

"The police show up for stolen gas cans?" Hester said.

"Oh, being a Yankee you wouldn't know about that, Hester... See, if a guy steals your gas can, he's saying he plans to burn down your house."

"I don't think they did that in Yonkers," Hester said.

"The guy who stole the can also put up a cross up in Tyrone's yard and hung a dead rat on it."

"Ohhhhh!" Melinda exclaimed. "That's voodoo!"

"Voodoo or stupidity," Maggie said.

"Once we pick up Scott and Carla Schmidt, we're ready to go," I said to Jake.

Driving south on Sycamore toward the Schmidts', we passed Dumbo striding along forthrightly in the twilight, buttocks sloshing in his baggy jeans.

"You guys ever get the feeling we're living in Toon Town?" Jake said. "I mean, we've got Dumbo and Uncle

Fester and Wonder Woman."

"Not to mention Kevin," Hester said. "Bugs Bunny."

"Bugsy Bunny," Jake corrected her. He turned to me. "Did I tell you about getting acquainted with that bozo I kept running into in the middle of the night last winter—the one with the crewcut and the big overcoat?"

"No."

"He was over on Pickett Street one morning about three, and I introduced myself. I asked him if he was in law enforcement. He said he didn't need law enforcement. He unbuttoned that coat of his and showed me his submachine gun."

"A submachine gun?"

"Yep. He had a big pocket sewn on the inside of that coat, and there it was."

"I've seen that guy around," Maggie said. "New York Doll said he's a cross-dresser."

Jake guffawed. "Why not? Who's New York Doll—another Toon?"

"You don't know Doll?" Hester said, "That tiny little prostitute."

"Y'all met our newest prostitute, Sparkle Plenty?" I put in. General hilarity in the van.

"If it's not too personal a question with your wife here, and all," Jake said, "where'd you meet her?"

"In the alley behind our house," I said, affecting naiveté. Hester elbowed me in the ribs, bringing laughter from the neighbors.

"I found out that thing Wonder Woman has in her belt purse is a handgun," Jake said. "She showed it to me the other night."

"Does everyone show you his or her gun, Jake?" Melinda asked.

"Well, it's kind of like, you show me yours, I'll show you mine. You gotta pack heat to get into the game."

Scott and Carla were waiting for us at the curb in front of their house.

"Jake, what's that wrecked car doing in front of your house?" Scott asked as he climbed into the van.

"It broke down there," Jake said. "Belongs to one of the drug-brats."

"Two wheels are missing," Carla said.

"Yeah, a couple guys came by one night, jacked the car up, and took 'em," Jake said. "I watched them do it."

"What happened to the windows?" Scott said.

"Somebody shot 'em out."

"After the car arrived at your place, or before?"

"After."

"How do you shoot windows out of a car without being noticed?" Hester said.

"Very carefully in the middle of the night while people are sleeping," Jake said. "You put a soda bottle over the gun muzzle. When the gun fires, it sounds about like a toy gun popping a cork."

"You know a lot about it, Jake," Melinda said.

"I'm very good at it," he said. "Oh look, there's Uncle Fester."

It was a muggy August night, but Fester wore his black turtleneck sweater and black trousers. He trudged along, hands clasped behind his back, eyes to the pavement.

"Toon City," Jake said.

We went up the hill on Jackson past my house en route to

the freeway. At the corner of Sycamore and Jackson, near the red brick house where Midnight Marvin was staying, Jake's headlights fell on a young black man who stared at us in the significant way of the street-dealer prepared to offer drugs.

"Seen him before?" Jake asked me.

"No."

Jake pulled the van alongside the fellow. "Where's your shit stashed, man?"

"I ain't sellin' no drugs."

"Every other scumbag around here is. What's wrong with you?"

"I'm waiting for a friend."

"Yeah, sure you are. You live at this corner?"

"No."

"Why would you be waiting for a friend here?"

"Who you, Inspector Colombo?"

"I live here. I'm interested in who's standing around on the street corners… What's your name?"

"Call me Ed."

"You new around here, Ed?"

"Old lady and me just moved down from Detroit."

"Ah, you're our guests then? You know, as a guest you always want to be on your best behavior. We'd like you to move off this corner."

Ed blew air through his lips contemptuously.

Jake reached under the seat of his van and came up with his Glock handgun which he pointed out the window at the guy on the corner. The Glock went click.

Ed from Detroit started up Jackson. Jake drove alongside him slowly. Turning into Tyrone's rooming house, Ed said, "You know where I can find work?"

Thirty or forty people from the neighborhood had shown up for the meeting at the mini-precinct in southwest Atlanta. About half were Lee Streeters. We sat on folding chairs arranged in classroom rank and file.

Our Councilman Lance Albright greeted us, expressed his profound concern with the difficulties we had been experiencing, and vowed his support. Then he introduced narcotics investigator Lieutenant Marc Angelo, a middle-aged white man with thick horn-rimmed glasses. Tie loose at the neck, sleeves of his white shirt rolled up, suspenders, gat-in-shoulder-holster—he looked disconcertingly like Woody Allen playing a hard-boiled detective. Baggy eyes intimated many late-night vigils. Angelo leaned forward on a rostrum at the front of the room, occasionally making notes as he listened to our stories.

Tyrone's rooming house came up frequently in the accounts of our problems. "That house should be your primary target. Absolutely no doubt about it," lawyer Bill Avery averred.

Angelo nodded agreement. "Busting that house would send a message to others working in the area. If what's going on there's as unrestrained as you say, busting them shouldn't be difficult.... It may take a while."

"Why's that?" Avery said.

"We have to do our own investigative work before we go into a house. We need to be pretty sure we'll find what we came for. If we screw up, judges won't usually issue a second search warrant."

"You should compare notes with Commander Gardner

of the Red Dogs," Avery said. "Jeff and I are old friends. We've been discussing that address. I don't know if he has anything planned."

"Yes, I'll do that," Angelo said. "We see each other nearly every day."

Mzz Boardman, who had been at Georgia Baptist Hospital in the weeks since her fall, died unexpectedly. Evidently there had not been any connection between her death and her broken collarbone.

"I think her poor old heart just gave out," Mzz Homer speculated as we sat on her porch before leaving for the funeral.

"If Maggie don't get here soon, we're going to be late," Mzz Grant said.

"It's only five minutes to the funeral home," Mzz Homer reassured her.

"When's all this dyin' gonna stop?" Mzz Grant said.

"May not," I said.

Mzz Homer grinned.

There had been a lot of dying lately: Skeeter, Terry, Mzz Boardman. The day before yesterday, Mr. Eggers, a well-larded white retiree, had suffered a fatal heart attack on his porch overlooking the Jackson-Confederate intersection. Riders on the 31 bus idling at the stop below Eggers' house had watched in horror as the tubby shirtless man pitched forward over his porch railing and somersaulted down the steep embankment. Mzz Grant, on the scene before the emergency medical crew arrived, reported Eggers had "strangled hisself … purple as a beet."

"You know," I said, gazing across the street, "from here Mzz Boardman's house looks even worse than it does from my place."

Mzz Grant agreed. "Pulls the neighborhood down."

"They kept it looking real nice while the mister was alive," Mzz Homer said. "After he passed, she couldn't keep it up."

"Didn't have no money," Mzz Grant said.

"Somebody'll come along now and fix it up," Mzz Homer said.

"I hope whoever it is don't plant bush and trees all over the place, way this one did," Mzz Grant said, looking at me askance—a fresh contribution to our ongoing, humorous dispute over my landscaping practices. Any shrub or tree added to a lawn was, as far as she could see, just one more place for a thief to hide.

"I never will know why y'all put that cherry tree in your front yard so I can't see what's going on over there," Mzz Grant said.

"I planted it so you couldn't see what was going on over there."

Mzz Homer chortled.

Mzz Grant reached for the paper cup on the table at her side. Holding back the ruffle at the neck of her Sunday-go-to-meeting dress, she drooled a loose saliva-tobacco mixture into the cup.

"Grant," Mzz Homer said, "you're pulling the whole neighborhood down with that Dixie cup of yours."

"Yeah," I said, "if we're going to bring this neighborhood around, we may have to renovate Mary Grant."

Mzz Grant was cackling. "No...Too late for that. If I gets too bad, just dig a hole in the ground and drop me in. I'll be getting on up the road to see my Maker."

"Better not go see him with tobacco drooling down your chin," Mzz Homer said. "He might get the wrong impression."

Mzz Grant thought it was hilarious.

A gunshot somewhere nearby made Mzz Homer blink.

"We can't bury you for a while yet, Mary," I said. "Too many funerals around here lately."

"Yeah," Mzz Homer agreed. "These collections for flowers are gettin' to be expensive."

"I'd like to have me a lot of roses at my funeral," Mzz Grant said.

"What are they these days, fifty dollars a dozen?" Mzz Homer said.

"Great big pile of 'em all over the coffin."

A small boy rapped his knuckles on the screened porch door.

"Whatcha need, baby?" Mzz Grant said, getting to her feet with a grunt.

"Gummy Bears."

"We all out of Gummy Bears, hon."

"Aw, I want me some Gummy Bears!"

"Come back tomorrow, we have 'em then."

"Want 'em now."

"I know, I know.... You come back."

Mzz Grant returned to her chair. "We're outta Butterfingers, too."

Mzz Homer nodded, indicating her awareness of this deficiency in inventory. "Sue's bringing both tomorrow."

It occurred to me that I had not checked on the progress of my Horizontal Drilling stock since I purchased it.

Maggie was coming up the hill wearing a gray suit and black heels. I had never seen her in anything but jeans before.

We set off for the funeral in my Honda, Maggie in the front seat with me, Mzz Grant and Mzz Homer in the back.

"Did y'all hear Chad and I got a live-in nanny?" Maggie said. "Ain't that special?"

"I can't think of anyone else around the neighborhood who has one," I said. "Of course, I can't think of anyone who needs one worse than you do, either... Where'd you get her?"

"She's been living right up the street from y'all... Bubbles."

"The stripper?"

"You know her?"

"Kevin talks about her... Is she getting out of show biz?"

"Yeah. She liked the money, but got tired of all the shit you put up with. After you dance, they escort you to your car, because some creep's probably following you... I danced for a while in New Orleans before I had five kids and my ass went bananas."

I was laughing.

"Well, honey, that's what happens."

"I was laughing at the way you put it."

"You watch, that'll end up in one of his stories," Maggie said.

"Is 'Bubbles' a nickname or stage name?"

"Nope, her real name. Bubbles McCarty."

"Who'd saddle a kid with a name like that?"

"Her old man runs a bubblesoap factory in Augusta. Biggest goddamn bubblesoap factory in the world, they say."

"How many are there?" I asked. "I mean, how many do

we need?"

"Well, my kids blow a lot of bubbles in the course of a summer," Maggie said. "Her old man is supposed to be filthy rich."

"If her father's rich, why's the girl have to get up on stage and dance buck naked?" Mzz Homer inquired.

"Daddy found out she liked black boys better than white and threw her out of the house." Maggie turned to me. "You know how New York Doll's always beggin' beers off us?"

"Yeah."

"She came to the door the other night and asked me for three. I thought that was a bit much, until she waved a five dollar bill under my nose. Five for three—not a bad deal, I thought, especially since I've probably given her a couple hundred dollars worth free. So I took the five for three. Next day, there's a guy at my door I never saw before tryin' to buy beer off me. I said, 'Hey, mister, this isn't a beer store.' Turns out he's an Alcohol and Firearms agent. Somebody was tryin' to get me arrested for selling beer without a license."

After the service at the funeral home, we drove down I-75 in the funeral cortege—it was more like a funeral race, actually—to the family burial plot in Jonesboro, Georgia, south of Atlanta. On the way home, after hours of sepulchral high-seriousness and eulogistic blarney, my riders and I were talkative.

Mzz Grant scoffed at Joe Boardman's nostalgic reminiscences of his aunt as one of the last of the Southern belles. "He never paid that woman one lick of attention, and then he gets up and talks all that crap."

Maggie said funerals, in general, were crap. A friend of hers forfeited a pre-paid vacation trip to Paris because her grandfather died the day her plane was to leave, and she had felt obligated to stay in Atlanta for the funeral. "She didn't even like the old guy! If he's dead, he's dead. Her not going to Paris sure as hell wouldn't bring him back. I'd have said, look, if you want me at the funeral, put the old boy on ice, and we'll have it after I'm back from the Eiffel Tower."

Mzz Grant and Mzz Homer were yukking it up in the back seat.

"Maggie," Mzz Grant said, "sometimes I don't know who crazier, you or me!"

"You know," I said, "I was thinking during the funeral that Mzz Boardman would make an excellent ghost."

I glanced in the rearview mirror at Mzz Grant, who had fixed me with one of her there-he-goes-again looks. "Mzz Boardman a ghost?"

"Well, ghosts often seem to be what's left of people who were very set in their ways. Maybe they spent forty or fifty years in the same house, and always followed the same routines. They're dead, but they still don't want to try anything new, so they stick around."

Mzz Grant got my drift. "That's old Boardman, for sure!...Where you git all this stuff?"

"He reads, Grant," Mzz Homer said. "If you'd read, you'd know something, too."

Mrs. Grant said she might consider take up reading if the world weren't about to end. As matters stood, it seemed like a lot of trouble.

Back home, I dialed the telephone number for Charles Scrip's "automated teller."

There was good news: Horizontal Drilling had gone up two cents since I bought my shares, and Seven Cities Gold was up a dime. I had made a cool two hundred-fifty dollars without lifting a finger. There was, however, a distressing detail in the report on my account: Somehow I had incurred a "debit balance" for precisely the amount that I paid Scrip for my Horizontal Drilling stock.

I was about to call Heidi at Scrip to ask about this when Mzz Grant knocked at my door. She had just run out of snuff. Could I give her a lift to the drugstore? I said I would.

We drove along Boulevard that really had been a boulevard when Atlanta was a sleepy provincial capital. An early twentieth century photograph showed two lanes of traffic divided by a median, and white women in long dresses with parasols promenading in the grass. But Boulevard had long been four narrow lanes of fast traffic. It was particularly busy that afternoon. Cars and trucks separated by a few feet flew past each other in the same and opposite directions.

Mzz Grant made a sound resembling a heartfelt OM which signaled, I knew from experience, her descent into prayer. Her lips were moving as she petitioned the powers that be for our safety on the road. Never having driven a car, with no idea how a little skill and effort might accomplish such a feat, she seemed to feel that only divine guidance could deliver an automobile safely from point A to point B. In this, as in many other matters, she tended to assign all competence to the Heavenly Father, including that portion of competence the Heavenly Father had apparently ceded to us: a spirituality rooted in ineptitude.

I parked the car in the parking lot of the drugstore, facing Boulevard, and sat there while Mzz Grant was shopping.

A full-bodied, barefoot young white prostitute toting a pair of sneakers in one hand came toward me. I had seen her working over in Cabbagetown, the neighborhood to our north. She sauntered listlessly, shoulders slumped, eyes to the ground. The body language expressed profound dejection. I wanted to see her face, and maybe because I was eyeing her intently, she looked up as she passed my car. Her eyes, red with tears, cried "Help!"—but not to me or anyone in particular. It was the cry for help of someone caught up in war or natural disaster who expected no response. And what could I do but sit there watching her through the window glass as if she were a fleeting image in a television report on a tragedy in some distant land?

Back in the 'hood, I braked the car in front of Mzz Grant's little shotgun house on Sycamore.

"Thank you, Lord Jesus!" she exclaimed throatily. Then she said, "What do I owe you?"

"You don't owe me anything, Mary."

"You have a blessed day, darlin'."

Back home, I called Heidi at Charles Scrip to ask about the "debit balance" in my account.

"Oh, you must be one of the victims," Heidi said offhandedly.

"Victims?"

She explained that each night the Scrip office gathered

together in a package all the checks and money orders from that day's business. A delivery service picked up the package and took it to a bank in Memphis. One day's package, including my money order, never made it to Memphis somehow, and could not be located.

"Is the delivery company liable?" I asked.

"No, and neither is Scrip, if you read the fine print of your contract. How did you pay for your stock?"

"Money order."

"The thing to do is stop payment on it, and bring us another."

The inconvenience of dealing with this problem was, in other words, to be mine, not Scrip's. I located the receipt for my money order. There was a form on the back to use in requesting cancellation of payment. Such a request would be honored if submitted in a "timely manner." A timely manner? The ambiguities were endless. I might not get my five hundred big ones back? There was a weird plausibility, given our idolatry of corporations, that none involved in this episode would be responsible for what had happened. Without saying a word or making a gesture, I found myself in that frame of mind in which people sink to their knees and petition the Heavenly Father for mercy.

That night on television, one of the network news magazines offered a piece on aluminum can-collecting as a homeless person's vocation on Manhattan.

There was an interview with a white woman identified simply as "Lucy" who had been making a living that way for years. The faded beauty of her face was photogenic, as the cameraman had realized. The close-up image of it filled the screen for several minutes as Lucy talked about her trade. She appeared to be in her fifties or early sixties, with cheekbones nearly as high and prominent as an Indian's, slightly concave cheeks, full lips that arched downward slightly in the corners.

It was only when the interviewer mentioned that Lucy had left Ohio after college in the 1960s to live in New York that I was aware I had been studying the face so intently because it had seemed vaguely familiar. Then I felt as if my hair were standing on end. Was this, in fact, Lucy Wagner, a college chum of mine, a painter who went to New York after college hoping to make connections in the New York art scene and (I had always assumed) to explore lesbian sexuality that attracted her? A mutual friend had told me in the early Seventies that she was still in New York, but I had heard nothing of her since then. It was possible that her life might have taken such a course.

I was not positive, though, that the face on the screen had been hers. In twenty or thirty years time, we are usually unrecognizable to one another.

ATLANTA'S BIG NEWS STORY in mid-August was the FBI sting that trapped a "dirty dozen" cops working out of our local precinct. They had assisted drug dealers in locating neighborhoods suitable for their operations—ours being one of them, no doubt—then helped them ward off invasive groups, while ignoring neighbors' complaints. The media called the sting the worst scandal in Atlanta police history.

But like the fire at Grandma Mitchell's, this revelation of corruption seemed to many of us a blessing in disguise. A housecleaning at the precinct might yield a new era of police probity and efficiency. Hope springs eternal.

A round little woman with freckles and an aureole of hair dyed bright orange appeared at the edge of my garden as I was picking beans one day to introduce herself as my new neighbor, Corky McGrew. Her father and she had just bought Mzz Boardman's house. They planned to start re-modeling it immediately.

"The house has changed hands already?" I said. "That usually takes a while."

"We don't mess around," Corky said, grinning. "Actually, we're buying it directly from Joe Boardman. The house has been in his name for years."

"I didn't know that."

"He and I went to school together. He's letting us go ahead and work on the house while the lawyer finishes the paper work."

We looked at the back of Mzz Boardman's house. So many coats of paint had flaked away, bare wood of the siding showed through at points. When Mzz Boardman had stepped out her back door onto the stoop to pour cooking slops over the railing, she'd had to step over a hole in the floorboards large enough to swallow her slender person. And when she had gone up and down her termite-infested back stairway, it swayed from side to side like a rope ladder.

"It's a dump," Corky said, "but it has all kinds of possibilities. You won't recognize it in a month."

"Is that a promise?"

She laughed. Her father and she renovated old houses for a living. She told me what they had paid for the house. The price struck me as exorbitant. But the McGrews made their living in real estate; it seemed more likely I had lost touch with the local housing market than that they were seriously mistaken about the value of Mzz Boardman's house.

"Once you've fixed up the house, you'll sell it again?"

"Nope, this one's mine. I'm queer by the way. I may as well tell you, I have a vision of the neighborhood as a haven for gays and lesbians." She smiled impishly.

"Reminds me of that banner in the Gay Pride Parade last year, 'Give us our rights, or we'll renovate your neighborhood.'"

"I remember it. That was funny."

"Welcome to the neighborhood."

I seemed to have passed her test.

Later that day, I drove up Boulevard intending to look at the for-sale advertisements taped in the front window at Toper Realty. But before I got to Toper's, what met my eye at the site of the former Amoco station was so unexpected I laughed out loud: The lot, a clay mire the last time I had seen it, had been repaved. At the back of the lot where the car wash had stood was a sparkling new canary-yellow pre-fabricated store with big, shiny plate glass windows, and a three-tiered red roof reminiscent of a Japanese pagoda roof. There were new gas tanks in front of the store—more of them than at the old station—and a glorious bank of public telephone kiosks along the Glenwood Avenue side of the lot. A sign facing Boulevard announced:

> COMING SOON FROM AMOCO
> "Split Second"
> Food, Beverages, Snacks, and More!

Well, but who could ask for anything more? Far from abandoning the neighborhood, Amoco was expanding its facilities! How silly it had been of me to imagine that Amoco would relinquish prime real estate so near a freeway exit! What, after all, were a few robberies, the occasional death of a cash register peon in the line of duty, and a modest redistribution of the national wealth?

There was more good news at Toper Realty. It was clear from the advertisements in the window that Corky and her father had not been mistaken about the current market value of houses like Mzz Boardman's. The 1990s flood of prosperity in Atlanta was raising all ships, including some decrepit dinghies. Junior mining and oil stocks? I should have bought another small house here five years ago!

Maggie and her daughter Angie came by one day to sit on my front porch with me.

"Something weird happened last night," Maggie said. "I was about to go to bed when three unmarked cop cars stopped in front of our house. They were from Zone 5, that precinct next over from ours? They'd heard from Zone 3 I knew Shit Boy, and they wanted me to show them where he hung out. I asked them what he'd done. They just said he was in big doo-doo. I got in one of the cars, and we drove around. I showed 'em where they were likely to find him. Is that cool or is that cool?"

One evening a truck backed into the side yard between my house and Corky's and dropped a dumpster with a foundation-shaking thud.

The next morning, a trio of bare-chested Mexican men with elastic sweatbands around their foreheads, garden spades in hand, and a boombox playing alien-sounding music in which accordions predominated, ascended to Corky's roof. Under a broiling sun, they hacked away at decayed shingles, heaving old roofing into the dumpster below.

The day after that, a second crew of Latinos showed up to install a new roof. Meanwhile, men wearing protective masks were hammering and crowbaring plaster and lathe from the 2x4 studs inside the house. Corky and her father weren't wasting any time.

I felt very cheerful suddenly about our prospects there on the urban frontier. The Lee Streeters, shaken from complacency by crimes in their immediate vicinity were "getting involved." We had Lieutenant Angelo and Commander Gardner working for us. The "dirty dozen" at the precinct were on the way out, presumably. Soon there would be not only food, beverages, and snacks at "Split Second," but more.

The aftermath of the fire at Grandma Mitchell's that wiped out a deteriorating situation was of a more ambiguous character. Wilson, looking down from his kitchen window at night, had seen the basketball-playing drug sellers going in and out of what remained of the house. Foul smells rising from the rubble when the summer sun hit it, and an occasional rat poking around, suggested the basketball players were now using the house as a latrine.

The burned-out house had also become, it seemed, a waystation in the local drug-distribution network. Hester was walking past Grandma Mitchell's en route to her bus stop one morning when two black youths, each with a package in hand, ran from the house and leapt into a car idling along the Oak Street side of the house. The driver, to prevent Hester's seeing the car's license tag, threw the car into reverse gear and backed all the way north to Lee Street.

It required only three phone calls to Narcotics for me to reach Lieutenant Marc Angelo. I described to him the drug activity at the burned-out house. Would it be possible, under the circumstances, for the city to speed up the demolition? Angelo was not sure that would be possible. There were legal considerations. The list of old houses awaiting demolition in Atlanta was a long one, and city funds and manpower were limited. Angelo said he would do what he could for us.

I had learned long ago that when a city worker said he would "see what he could do," nothing would happen. I telephoned Bill Avery and described for him the situation at Grandma Mitchell's. Avery said he would take up the matter with City Councilman Albright

One morning a week later, there was a bulldozer in Grandma Mitchell's front yard. A crowd of neighbors had gathered to watch the action: Wilson, Maggie and two of her children, Bubbles the nanny, John the Drunk, Uncle Fester, Dumbo, and Simone. The bulldozer operator clobbered blackened portions of the house still standing with the scoop arm of the machine.

"Y'all hear about Sparkle Plenty?" Maggie said, as I joined the group.

I hadn't.

"That old guy she stayed with in Cabbagetown shot her in the head and killed her last night, then turned the gun on himself."

The trembling started again. My mouth was bone dry.

A dump truck filled with terra cotta-colored Georgia clay rumbled downhill, braking at the corner and backing into Grandma Mitchell's lot. An hydraulic lift raised the front of the truck bed. Fill dirt slid through the hinged back door of the truck into the dugout where foundation posts for Grandma Mitchell's house had stood.

Robert Smith, the bearded city building inspector who oversaw demolition and construction in the area, drove up in his lemon-yellow Geo convertible. Maggie and I were chatting with Smith when a group of young black men associated with the drug trade, led by their totem rottweiler, came toward us from a house on Oak Street. It looked like a tribal war party setting out for battle. Long strands of gold chains swung at the neck of the leader of the group who held the dog leash.

"What's this?" Smith muttered.

"Stupidity on parade," Maggie said.

"Gotta match?" one of the teenagers asked as they swept past us—i.e., *We gonna burn yo house down mothafuka.*

The newcomers formed a discrete spectator group at the corner. The guy with the gold chains ran up the antenna of a cellphone self-importantly. Eyeing the bulldozer at work, and us, he filed a report on the situation to some interested party.

Why were they so upset? Did they suppose the city would let the burned-out house stand there indefinitely?

When I returned home, a dead pigeon lay on the walk near my porch steps. Depositing a dead animal or bird at the house of a "snitch" was a form of intimidation neighborhood gangs employed commonly. I was contemplating the pigeon with the intensity of an augur when Sid the tomcat came around the side of my house, dug his teeth into pigeon feathers with a proprietary air, and made off across the street with his meal.

Maggie and Kevin were coming up Jackson from the scene of the demolition toward my porch when a brouhaha broke out behind them. They paused to look back. John the Drunk was complaining that one of the young men from the drug house was not showing him "respect."

The youths were laughing at him. "You don't deserve no respect, pussy-nigger."

John put up his dukes. "OK, let's see whatcha got! Let's see whatcha got!"

"John, shut up," Simone said. "You're drunk and you're gonna get hurt."

"Woofwoofwoofwoofwoof," commented the huskies from across the street.

John stepped toward his adversary and seemed intent on throwing the first punch, but tripped and fell down.

Maggie was shaking her head as she and Kevin came up the walk to my porch. "He'll go on like that until he either falls asleep or someone punches him out."

"Pretty early in the day for him to be that drunk isn't it?" I remarked.

"Hell, he ain't never been in bed!" Kevin said.

They sat down side by side on the porch railing.

"John's a crazy fool," Maggie said, "but, you know, he's the only one of them I really trust."

"Tell him what happened up to the drugstore that time," Kevin said.

"Oh, that," Maggie said. "It was right after Christmas last year. The drugstore on Boulevard was having a sale on Christmas junk? Jay and I rode up on bicycles to check it out. Turned out, the sale ended the day before, but I know Shirley at the checkout. She told me they'd just thrown a lot of Christmas stuff into the dumpster. We went around back to have a look. There was all sorts of crap I could use next Christmas, but we wouldn't be able to carry much of it on our bicycles. John was doing some plumbing for me at the house that day—he's a good plumber, by the way, if he's sober. I called home and told him to get in our pickup and haul ass over to the drugstore."

"You let him drive your truck?" I said.

"He was sober. He crawled right into the dumpster and was handin' stuff out to us when I remembered I'd left a five dollar bill in the glove compartment? When John wasn't looking, I snuck a peek. It wasn't there."

"Yeah, guess who took it," Kevin said.

"We finished loading up," Maggie said. "Jay and I went back into the store to thank Shirley. Then I told John that we were gonna go over to Burger King for lunch. Did he want to come along? I was buyin'. Yeah, sure, he'd come. We all got in the truck. I was driving. 'John,' I said, 'there's a five-dollar bill there in the glove compartment. Would you mind handing it to me?' He opens the glove compartment, and there's the five, right where I put it. He hands it over with this shit-eatin' smile. 'John,' I said, 'you took that five and then put it back, didn't you?' He said, 'Yes, m'am, I did.' I asked him why he put it back. He said, 'I couldn't bite the hand what feeds me.'"

Dump trucks loaded with fill dirt came past my house, one after the other.

Ketchup Robinson's mustard-colored old Chevette came rattling and smoking up Jackson from Confederate Avenue. There was a grinding of steel-on-steel at the Oak-Jackson intersection as Ketchup struggled to get the car into low gear for the ascent of the hill. Before he had succeeded in this task, the car rolled to a halt. Kevin leaned over the porch railing, nose pointed like a hunting dog's at the car.

"See that guy in the back with the hat over his face? That's Shit Boy!"

"Does look like him, don't it?" Maggie agreed. "They're moving him around from one car to another, one apartment to another. He knows the cops are after him."

"Should we call 911?" I put in.

"She-it," Kevin said, "time them assholes get here, he could be in Alabama."

"Would the car go that far?"

The Chevette chugged up the hill, and had only just turned onto Boulevard when a squad car appeared serendipitously at the foot of the hill. Maggie and Kevin leapt off my porch and ran down the street, waving their arms to get the officer's attention.

The patrol car turned up Jackson and came toward us. The officer was none other than our fair beat cop, the reborn Atalanta Timmons with her officer's cap perched jauntily atop her bun of hair.

"Yellow Chevette!" Kevin barked, pointing up the hill. "Shit Boy! Yellow Chevette! Ketchup!"

Timmons contemplated Kevin as she might have a dog barking.

Maggie provided Timmons with a less breathless account of the Shit Boy-sighting. The squad car sped up Jackson toward Boulevard.

"Timmons again," Maggie said. "Well, I guess she's better than nothing."

"You'd be a good cop, Maggie," Kevin said.

"Hell, I patrol more around here than the cops do, as it is."

"Timmons screws with a fireman," Kevin said.

Maggie's gray eyes smoldered. "Now Yellow Dog, how would you possibly know that."

"Everbody knows it."

"I heard she's engaged to a fireman," I put in.

"My brother's engaged," Kevin said. "He's gettin' married up in South Carolina next month. His fiancee got even bigger knockers on her than Timmons."

"White girl is she?" Maggie said.

Kevin nodded yes, missing the irony. "They're gonna have a cowboy weddin'."

"What's a cowboy weddin'?" Maggie asked.

"You know, everbody wears cowboy hats and boots and stuff."

"Why would they want to do that?"

Dimple-cheeked Kevin grinned and shrugged. "Mumma wants 'em to. I'm gonna be the best man.... What's a best man do?"

"Not a helluva lot," Maggie said. "Mainly stands around and holds the ring."

"Aw, she-it, gonna be borin'!" Kevin shut his eyes and did a noisy imitation of a person snoring.

"What you gonna wear, Kevin?" Maggie asked.

"Mumma got me this cowboy shirt with sparkles all over the front.... Faggot shirt's what it is."

"Maybe you can get some wear out of it later if you dance at the gay club," I said. "It would match your jockstrap."

"Dance at a gay club?" Maggie said.

I explained.

"You wanna be a stripper, Kevin?" Maggie said, looking at him incredulously.

"Hell, yes, for two hundred a night! All the faggots do is stick bills in your jockstrap. Ain't gonna catch no AIDS from that."

Maggie and I exchanged a look.

"Y'all hear about that black faggot stole Don and Lee's van?" Kevin said.

It was news to Maggie and me.

"They picked him up on Ponce de Leon last night and brought him home. He wanted a lift back to Ponce this morning. They wouldn't give him none, so he stole the keys to the van and took off. Ain't seen him or the van since."

A patrol car driven by a black male officer appeared now at the foot of the hill where Timmons had been earlier. Kevin bolted from the porch to the curb. The car idled at the corner for a time, then crept through the intersection past Maggie's house—only to reappear a few moments later laying rubber as it careened around the corner at Confederate and Jackson with its blue flasher turning. It raced up the hill past us.

"Sumpin goin' on!" Kevin exulted. Maggie went down to the street to join him.

Now there was a police helicopter putt-putting over Grant Park at the top of the hill. Kevin and Maggie were gazing uphill toward the sound when Angie came up Jackson on foot. Seeing that I had noticed her, she put a silencing forefinger to her lips, and tip-toed toward her mother and Kevin at the curb. She reached around her mother's waist and dug her fingers into ribs: "Cootchie-cootchie!"

"Goddamn it, Angie! How many times I gotta tell you not to do that! I'm gonna have a heart attack one of these days!"

The triumphant Angie grinned at Kevin, anticipating his approval of her prank. Kevin retreated from the curb to my porch and stood beside me, as if for protection.

Angie came up into the yard in our direction. She only had eyes for Kevin. How much they looked alike, despite the discrepancy in their ages! The same wideset eyes and dirty blond hair, the same coltish wildness about the face. Looking at each other must have been for them almost like looking into a mirror. Standing beside Kevin, I was aware that, as far as The Female was concerned, I was a goner, of no consequence whatsoever. I might as well have been a ghost. Not a bad feeling, actually: clean, cool, transparent. I felt as if I could walk through sheetrock, in and out of points of view.

Not being able to stand the heat of the girl's gaze any longer, Kevin said, "Gonna get me a Butterfinger," and strode across the street to Mzz Homer's. Opening the screened door there, he cast a quick, leery look back at the dangerous hoyden in my yard.

"He's so cute," Angie murmured, as if out of a dream, to no one particular.

A motor scooter carrying a black youth came buzzing down the hill.

"Shit Boy!" Maggie yelped. He gave us the finger as he flew past, his dreadlocks flying out behind him.

"Timmons!" Maggie screamed to the heavens, "where the fuck are you when we need you!"

In the intersection at the foot of the hill, Shit Boy executed a right turn into Oak so fast and low, the scooter nearly went out from under him. As if in response to Maggie's anguished cry, down the hill came Timmons in hot pursuit! Around the corner from Jackson into Oak she went, a second squad car right behind her!

"Yeah!...Yeah!...Yeah!" Maggie enthused. She leapt repeatedly into the air with her arms raised in a way that intimated cheerleading somewhere in her past.

Kevin leapt off Mzz Homer's porch. "They're gonna catch his ass! They're gonna catch his ass!"

The helicopter came our way now, swooping over my house low enough to rattle windowpanes. Squad cars zoomed around in nearby streets.

Then, dense, prolonged silence.

The helicopter regained altitude and headed off to the south away from the park.

In a little while, Timmons turned her squad car off Confederate Avenue into Jackson, drove uphill at a leisurely pace, and pulled to the curb in front of my house. She removed her officer's cap and lay it on the car seat. Looking at herself in the car mirror, she patted a few stray hairs into place as we gathered around the squad car.

"The perpetrator, B.B. Moore, is in custody," she announced matter of factly.

"Shit Boy's in jail!" Kevin rejoiced. "D-a-a-a-am!"

"Good work, Timmons," Maggie said.

"Congratulations," I added. "What happened?"

"The perpetrator was in the Chevette you people saw." Timmons smiled slightly. "It broke down right in front of the precinct over in the Park."

Kevin found it hilarious. "Ah-ha-ha-ha-ha-ha-ha-ha-ha-ha. Old Ketchup's car!"

"Moore left the car," Timmons said.

"Shit Boy," Kevin corrected her.

"Moore," Timmons continued, "jumped from the car. Sergeant Snyder was just leaving the precinct and recognized him. He knew there were warrants outstanding against him, and chased him into Summerhill on foot."

"Shit Boy was on a scooter when he came past here," Maggie said.

"They say that belongs to a friend of his."

"He ain't gonna be shittin' on your porch no more, Maggie!" Kevin said. "His porch-shittin' days is done!"

Timmons placed her police cap back atop her bun of hair.

"Well, you did real good, Timmons," Maggie said.

"It's my job," Timmons said.

"Not bad for a girl," Kevin said.

Angie kicked Kevin in the butt and raced down the hill, looking over her shoulder in hopes he would give chase.

That night, I found myself thinking about the little band of black youths with the rottweiler that had come down Oak Street while the house was being demolished. Their displeasure at what was happening had seemed inexplicable to me earlier. Now I thought I understood: They had used the house for their own purposes before and after the fire, and felt their use of it had established their right to it. Having no personal experience of property ownership or its legal rights and obligations, and probably no knowledge of them, either, and seeing law and government as the means by which people with money deprived poor black people of what they needed to live—the youths regarded the arrival of the city-sponsored bulldozer as the invasion of the enemy.

The point of view had a certain cogency.

ESTER AND I, STARTING UP JACKSON toward Jake and Jill's house for a party Saturday night, paused to observe the work done on Mzz Boardman's house. There was fresh white paint on the siding, a new gray roof. Posts tapered gracefully from narrower tops to broader bases supporting the porch roof, replacing the prosaic rectangular boxes that had leaned slightly. We could see a corner of a sun-deck under construction at the back of the house.

Corky waved to us from a stepladder in the front window of the house as we passed.

The Machts' patio party was one of those big, amorphous, middle class affairs that throws into the drink to sink or swim a retired insurance executive from Milwaukee, a bearded neighborhood activist, a professor of musicology at a black college, a video editor from Cable News Network, and a pert youngish widow on the make, voluble after several drinks about her ancestors who came over on the Mayflower.

Hester and I left the party at eleven and walked the short distance down Boulevard to Jackson.

We had just made the turn down our street when the scene in front of Tyrone's rooming house made me wish we had gone home some other way. There were a half dozen police cars, marked and unmarked, facing both uphill and downhill, some parked hastily at odd angles to curbs. The rooming house regulars, including Tyrone and Mike wrists pinioned behind their backs by handcuffs, sat elbow to elbow on the curb in front of the house. They were being frisked one by one and inserted into a police wagon.

Mike's eyes met mine briefly—hostilely.

Well, I thought, there goes the conclusion of the story he had been telling me, not to mention the five dollars I had advanced him.

Within the hour, a group of neighbors (white neighbors) had assembled on my front porch: Wilson, Kevin, Maggie, Bubbles, and Angie. Corky McGrew, having noticed our assemblage, came from her porch to join us. I introduced her to the others.

"I've never seen so many police cars in one place at one time," Corky said. "What was that all about?"

"Got their asses busted," Kevin said. "Cops turned out the lights and locked the door."

"That's a crack house up there," Maggie explained.

"It is?" Corky said.

"Welcome to the neighborhood, Corky," Maggie said.

Corky laughed nervously. "Does that kind of thing happen a lot around here?"

"Not nearly often enough," Maggie said. "Fact is, ain't never happened, far as I know."

"Tyrone's been askin' for it," Kevin opined.

"I wouldn't sound so high and mighty, Yellow Dog,"

Maggie said. "If you'd been up there tonight, your ass would be in the slammer, too."

Corky laughed nervously.

"She-it," Kevin said. "I knowed them cops was snooping around. Ain't no cop ever take me alive."

Wilson was struggling to swallow laughter.

The phone rang in the house. Bill Avery from Lee Street was on the line. Commander Gardner of the Red Dogs had just phoned to tell him of the bust at the rooming house. "He said they took twenty-two people out of that little house. Can you imagine?"

"There's been a lot of traffic there lately."

"I think we've made a start in getting this thing under control," Avery said.

"Well, let's hope so. Gardner say anything about what quantity of drugs they found? What happens next might depend a lot on that."

"I asked him that, but he didn't know. He wasn't at the bust himself."

I hoped we had not just witnessed the equivalent of another police sweep. A lot of what police did reminded me of theater. It did not require a very great change of perspective to see squad cars, guns, badges, and uniforms as props and costumes. There were certain similarities between these street dramas of theirs, and allegorical plays depicting struggles of Good and Evil the Church had put on in medieval towns.

"Who are those people?" Corky was asking Maggie as I rejoined my neighbors on the porch. She pointed to a second gathering of humanity—black—under the streetlight at the foot of the hill.

"Friends and family of the perps," Maggie said. "White folks are supposed to scare easy. They're trying to spook us."

"I scare pretty easy," Corky admitted.

"Me, too," said Bubbles.

Corky put her arm around Bubbles' waist.

"Oh, it's mainly woofing," Maggie said.

"Woofing?" Corky said.

"You know—woofwoofwoof!"

"Some of them suckers'll blow you away without thinking twice about it," Kevin said.

"They talk as if they would," I said.

"Talk shit, I seen 'em do it over in Eastlake Meadows. Some of them guys is crazy."

Mookie and Simone, en route down Jackson to join the crowd at the corner, looked our way sourly as they passed under the streetlight in front of my house.

"Mookie nooky," said Kevin.

"Well, looks like the whores are pissed anyway," Maggie said. "We must be doing sumpin right."

"Cops run off their customers," Kevin said.

"You have prostitutes around here?" Corky said.

"Oh hell yes," Maggie said. She turned to me. "You know that guy Taylor lives up on Boulevard near Jake?"

"No."

"He had this old black funeral hearse parked behind his garage? He used to fool around with it, try to get it going, but he gave up on it. It was just sitting there. Cops come by the other night and ask if he's running a whore house. He didn't know what they were talking about. Some prostitutes had got into the hearse. They were servicing customers in it."

I was laughing.

"Had it all fixed it all up with plush carpeting and red velvet curtains. Taylor threw the girls out. Next day their pimp comes around and gives him five hundred bucks for the hearse."

Someone in the crowd at the foot of the hill had gone for the totem rottweiler. Now, with the dog leading the way, the opposition party came up Jackson slowly toward us, pausing under the streetlight in front of my house to stare at us.

"Bark, Tyson, bark," someone in the crowd murmured.

Tyson dropped to his rump, thrust one leg into the air like a ballerina, and gnawed at a flea on his inner thigh. Muffled laughter from the group as they continued slowly up the hill.

"In two weeks," Maggie said, "we put away Shit Boy and Tyrone's crowd. By god, I'm throwin' a victory party! We can't afford it, Chad'll kill me. I don't care, I'm doing it. Next Saturday night in our yard. Y'all are invited. Bring your own drinks, I'll do the rest."

"I'll foot half the bill," I said.

Maggie and I exchanged high-fives.

"You gonna have it in your yard?" Kevin said dubiously. "Them drug boys hang out at Mookie's cross the street."

"You think I give a flying fuck, Kevin?"

"The drug boys are likely to be in jail," I pointed out.

"Yeah, but they got friends," Kevin said.

"If those suckers think they can take over this neighborhood," Maggie said, "they gonna have to do it over my dead body." She knocked on wood.

"I think it's going to be more interesting here than it was up in Buckhead," Corky said.

"Is that where you come from?" Maggie said. "We lived up there two years, I damn near died of boredom."

Monday morning, hoping to determine what quantity of drugs the raid on the rooming house had netted, I put in a call to Commander Gardner of the Red Dogs.

The officer who answered the phone told me Gardner was at a law enforcement convention in Philadelphia. No one else on duty could, or would, answer my question.

So I called Lieutenant Marc Angelo in Narcotics, who surely would have the information I wanted. While I waited for someone in Narcotics to answer the phone, an old high school cheer was going through my mind:

> *Albright, Albright, he's our man.*
>   *If he can't do it—*
> *Gardner can.*
> *Gardner, Gardner, he's our man*
>   *If he can't do it—*
> *Angelo can.*
> *Angelo, Angelo, he's our man...*

Amazingly, Angelo was not only in his office, but willing to take a phone call.

I assumed he knew about the bust at Tyrone's rooming house?

"Bust?" Angelo said. "What bust?"

I described the action in the 'hood Saturday night.

"That may have screwed up the investigative work we were doing," he said accusatorily—as if my neighbors and I had double-crossed him. I had the uncomfortable feeling I might have just given him a pretext for ignoring our situation.

"You told us you'd be in touch with Commander Gardner about the rooming house," I said.

Heavy silence at the other end of the line.

Heavy silence all that week in the neighborhood, too. Silence, and August heat and drought. My front yard's botanical potpourri devolved into its annual late-summer straw phase. Auto and pedestrian traffic in the 'hood had virtually ceased after the bust. No peripatetic whores. *No Dadada DOOOOOM!* No late night basketball on Oak Street. No cars along curbs with hoods up for make-believe car repairs, or make-believe tire-changings, to cover street-selling.

About the only sounds Jackson Street produced that week were air conditioner condensers kicking in; the ice cream wagon with its endlessly repetitive, vaguely sinister, electronic rendering of "Pop Goes the Weasel"; and the nailguns of sheetrock installers zapping studs next door at Corky's.

The big bust at Tyrone's had eliminated not only undesirable behavior in the 'hood, but very nearly behavior itself. The ambiance was Knoxville, 1915. I didn't like it. I had no idea that so much of the life of my surroundings depended on the rooming house.

I read a lot of Juvenal.

Kevin's estimation of the situation as he sat glumly on my porch Wednesday afternoon agreed with mine: "Borin'!"

He pointed at my yellowed lawn. "That wouldn't happen if you had zoysia grass."

Thursday, there was good news from the financial sector: My request to stop payment on my money order to Charles Scrip had been honored. I purchased a replacement money order and delivered it to Heidi. Horizontal Drilling was up another two cents, and Ahah! Silver, in Chile, six cents. I made a four-hundred-dollar profit that day.

I went out for a walk in the afternoon. Up near the Jackson-Boulevard intersection, the homeless men were not sitting in front of the split-level house as I passed. But across the street, Bill Clinton was at his window. "Have a nice day," I called to him.

Clinton said nothing until I reached the top of the hill, when he called after me, "Fuck you, asshole!"

Alas, Clinton had fallen in with a bad crowd.

I mentioned the transformation of Clinton's vocabulary as Wilson and I were drinking beer on his porch Thursday night.

"Yeah, he called me a sonofabitch when I went past on my bicycle the other day," Wilson said. "That woman I sold him to seemed so nice."

He hadn't known about the homeless men who had broken into the vacant apartment across the street.

"I heard a lot of parrot jokes while I had him. There's one about a woman with a bird who cusses. She says to him, 'Look, either you stop that, or I'm going to put you in the fridge.' The birds keeps it up, so she opens the freezer door and pops him in. Ten minutes later, she opens up. The parrot's got his feathers all fluffed out. She says, 'Well, did you learn your lesson?' The parrot says, 'God, what did the chicken do?!'"

Maggie and several of her children came up the street on foot. Maggie reported that Bubbles and the children were working on a big paper banner for the victory party Saturday night. It would stretch all the way across the front of her porch.

New York Doll knocked at my door that night. She had cast aside her crutch and her eye patch, and seemed more or less her old self.

"Where you been, Doll?"

"Missed me?"

"Well, it hasn't been quite the same around here without you."

"I been in Cabbagetown. Have to go over there to find johns since they shut down Tyrone."

"Must be more competition over there."

"Yeah, there is. I got in a cat fight last night." She raised her face to reveal fingernail slashes running down her neck.

She took a five dollar bill from her pocket and handed it to me.

"What's this for?"

"Three beers."

Five for three had a familiar ring to it.

Refusing the five, I gave her one beer, free. She handed me a new "Report from the Street."

SICK AND TIRED

I am truly sick and tired of lying, cheating, stealing, using people as objects not individuals, and not being respectful. I am mental exhaust.

When I moved here from Harlem, I had a dream of a better life for myself, a slower pace. But since I came here, I have had five black eyes, bruised ribs, a divorce, lower back pain, and mental instability. In all truth, I am fucked up in Atlanta. I have about had it with these country boys who work off all their problems beating up women. But though I keep telling myself I have had enough ass-whipping, I know there will be more of the same until I give up the crack.

It has been four days since I had even a beer, not to mention crack. I have been Miss Goody Twoshoes. Which is good. But it's only what they call a "dry spell," and I know it won't last. Truth is, I will probably be on the street high all this weekend.

To get off the crack for good, I will have to change my playground and playmates. I don't have strength to do it myself. God will have to do this for me, and I know He can, because He is all-powerful. Amen.

Variation on a theme of Mzz Grant's.

News from Municipal Court enlivened local conversation Friday. Shit Boy made his first appearance before a judge. Maggie and Kevin, eager to see their nemesis brought to grief, were in court. They came home with breathless accounts of the charges against Shit Boy, which were more numerous and serious than any of us had suspected: sixteen counts of armed robbery in the Virginia-Highlands area of Atlanta, two counts of aggravated assault (including the attack on Maggie's son), and one case of kidnapping.

Shit Boy, nineteen, would be tried as an adult in the state Superior Court of Fulton County. It seemed likely he would do hard time. Informed that he could not stay with his mother while awaiting trial, he wept. His mother had pleaded with the judge, "But Your Honor, boys will be boys."

Saturday afternoon, I was strolling through Grant Park beside the Atlanta Zoo when I observed through a tall chainlink fence this tableau vivant: Two giraffes facing away from me stood side by side, their legs splayed outward at the knees like Chippendale tables. In front of the giraffes were two bookend ostriches, tail feathers-to-tail feathers. Off to one side, a third giraffe looked at me with large, unblinking brown eyes through tree leaves on which it had been grazing. No one moved.

Then, as if someone had thrown a switch, or a huge mobile had caught a wind, all the creatures moved simultaneously: The giraffe pair pirouetted in opposite directions, one clockwise, one counter-clockwise, and came around to face me. Giraffe three crossed to the opposite side of my visual field. The two ostriches exchanged places. Then the whole company halted again, like a marching band in a new formation awaiting applause.

Everything had changed—and nothing.

Hester and I had just set off downhill toward Maggie's for the victory party late Saturday afternoon when Corky McGrew caught up with us from behind.

"Good news! My Dad's buying that vacant lot at Oak and Jackson where the fire was. He's going to put up a brand new house!"

"That is good news," Hester agreed. "We're going to be very respectable-looking around here one of these days."

The banner Bubbles and the children had fashioned stretched across Maggie's porch roof:

USE COCAINE AND LOSE YOUR BRAIN.

There were smells of meat cooking. Maggie's children and their neighborhood friends were in the front yard gathered around a big jar of bubble soap. They waved their arms through the air in wide arcs, releasing showers of bubbles into the air. Bubbles the nanny, ringlets of honey-blond hair cascading down her bare shoulders, bent over the younger children showing them how to work this magic.

Maggie, working over a barbecue grill on her screened porch, opened the porch door and raised her spatula in greeting. Kevin, Chad, Mzz Homer, Mzz Grant, and Mzz Bevins (a widow living next door to Maggie) occupied folding chairs on the porch.

Next door, Uncle Fester gazed from his porch at the assembled flesh.

Bubbles organized the bubble-blowers into a makeshift choir which chanted:

> No more drugs,
> No more pain,
> We don't want
> Your crack cocaine!

The adults applauded the performance.

"Ain't that just cute as hell," I heard a black man's voice say, with utter sincerity. I looked across the street to where John the Drunk, a boozy grin on his face, sat on the curb in front of Mookie's house. At his side was a lean, expressionless, young man who talked into a cellphone.

"One, two, three," shouted Bubbles, and the choir chanted:

Drug-dealer, drug-dealer
You're not nice.
We're onto you
Like white on rice!

"That one certainly resonates," Hester whispered to me.

Carla and Scott Schmidt were coming our way along Oak Street from Pickett.

"Y'all hear there was another arrest?" Maggie said. "Shark's in the Fulton County Jail."

"How'd that happen?" I asked.

"I put him there," Maggie said. "I was truckin' down Boulevard yesterday. Who should I see sitting on a wall across from the penitentiary but your friend and mine. That boy looked terrible. He'd been on the street for days, I think. He was so happy to see someone he knew, I don't think he even remembered stealing my cart. Came right over to the truck. I told him I was out for a ride, he want to come along? Sure, he did! I opened the truck door, and he got right in. Smell?! Lord, he was dead meat. I didn't have my warrant for him in the truck, so I drove over here and got it, and a beer for Shark, and then I went straight to the precinct."

"Shark didn't mind that?" Hester said.

"Honey, he was a happy camper sitting there sucking on his Bud. Wait a minute, I gotta flip these burgers."

A late-model BMW drove up in front of Tamika/Tamara Thomson-Thomas-Tomasso's house a few houses down Jackson from the Oak Street intersection. A solidly-built, bald black man wearing a suit got out of the car, went up the steps to the house, and pressed a doorbell button. Gazing about idly as he waited for the door to open, he noticed my attention fixed on him.

"So where was I?" said Maggie, returning to the yard.

"You were driving Shark over to the police station," Hester said.

"Yeah, so I parked right out front and went inside. I gave the desk sergeant the warrant. He said, 'What's this?' I said, it's a warrant for the guy outside. He said, 'Outside where?' I said, in my truck. 'No way,' he said. I told him to come see. The cop asked Shark if his real name was Russell Cryder. Shark said it was. The cop handcuffed him. Shark asked me if I could see to it they kept him in jail at least a month. I think he figured it would take him that long to get straight."

The guy who appeared regularly at Tamara/Tamika's house dressed like a construction worker opened the front door of the house for the man driving the BMW. The two exchanged a few words in the doorway. Both looked my way before entering the house.

Suddenly, I thought I understood: The guy who dressed like a construction worker and drove the Ford Escort was a prosperous middle-level dealer who dressed inconspicuously and drove an old car to divert attention from himself, as many of his kind did. He supported Tamara-Tamika in a style to which she aspired. No, they would not have wanted to mingle with the neighbors; and yes, Tamika-Tamara would certainly have wanted to be a member of our telephone network of concerned citizens.

Something else occurred to me: Before I had begun receiving the prank telephone calls, I had given my phone number not only to the assistant pastor of the AME church, but to Tamika-Tamara.

New York Doll came up Oak Street from Pickett to the south looking like a ten-year-old boy in her jeans, T-shirt, and baseball cap. She paused in front of Maggie's house to read the children's banner.

"Now they tell me!" she said in her raspy voice.

"Hey, Doll, want a hamburger?" Maggie called from the porch.

"Yeah, and a cold one!…Mr. Author and Mrs. Author. I want you to be the first to know I'm going back to south Jersey to start a new life. My uncle bought me a plane ticket and signed me up for a drug rehab program."

"Well, that's good news, Doll," Hester said.

"Nice to know your in-laws look out for you," Doll said. "I need to get out of Atlanta, change my life."

"You've had some bad times here," Hester said.

"I don't think I'll be alive much longer if I stay around. I want y'all to know how much I appreciate your being good to me."

"When are you leaving?" I asked.

"When I get clearance from my parole officer. Til then, I'm trying to stay straight. I'm having trouble makin' ends meet, though. Suppose y'all could lend me five to get a place to stay tonight?"

I hesitated. Hester, whose experience of these appeals was less extensive than mine, reached into her purse and came up with a five.

Maggie handed Doll a hamburger wrapped in a paper napkin, and a can of beer.

"God bless you all," Doll said. "You are the Lord's people."

She went off up the hill. She paused in front of our house to munch on her sandwich and swill a little beer from the can, then continued on her way.

"Third time I've heard that bit about New Jersey," Maggie said. "We're ready to eat." She began shepherding guests onto the porch.

Bubbles was screwing the lid on an "economy size" bottle of "Barrels of Bubbles."

"Is that the stuff your Dad makes?" I asked.

"You know about that?"

"Maggie told me."

"Yeah, he's a sonofabitch, but he makes great bubble soap. I used to buy the stuff by the case when I was dancing …I had a bubble machine."

"And you danced to 'I'm Forever Blowing Bubbles'?"

"How'd you know that?"

I tapped a finger against my forehead to indicate the source of my psychic powers.

Children and adults crowded onto the long narrow porch and sat knee-to-knee on folding chairs to eat hamburgers and hot dogs, German potato salad, cole slaw, and big slabs of chocolate cake with vanilla ice cream on the side.

Mzz Grant said to me, "You know what you said about Mzz Boardman being a ghost? Geraldine and me seen this funny light out front of her house last night after the workman left. Didn't we, Geraldine?"

"It gave me goosebumps," Mzz Homer said. "I'll bet anything she's upset by the way they're changing the house."

I was sorry I had ever brought up the matter of ghosts.

Bubbles and Corky were deep in conversation.

"Did you invite Fester and his wife?" I asked Maggie.

"Yeah, but they don't party."

"What do they do?" Hester asked.

"Nothin'," Maggie said. "Fester's hiding something in his past, I think. Everything they own's in her name. The only name he gives out is 'Fester.'"

The children, having gulped down their food, were back in the yard blowing bubbles, or tooling around the corner of Oak and Jackson on bicycles and tricycles in the twilight. In the now more ample space of the porch, the adults leaned back in their chairs and stretched their legs while Maggie and Angie served coffee. Kevin got his first, from Angie, with a very pretty smile.

"Y'all know what I heard today?" Kevin said. "Mookie got AIDS."

"Oh Jesus, where did you hear that?" Maggie said.

"Simone."

"If it's true, half the men in the block could have it, too," Maggie said.

"Y'all hear about Mookie and Dumbo?" Kevin said.

We hadn't.

Antonio, an enterprising black youth from the 'hood who had seen a potential in Dumbo no one else did, had developed a scheme: Dumbo would steal baseball cards from the hobby shop on Boulevard, and Antonio would fence them. Last week, Dumbo had proven surprisingly light-fingered, filching three hundred dollars worth of classic baseball cards. Antonio had rewarded him with twenty crisp, new one dollar bills.

Delighted by the texture of the bills, and the thickness of the stack, Dumbo had traipsed down Jackson to Mookie's to show off his newfound wealth. Mookie, in serious need of a hit, was home alone when Dumbo knocked on her door. When she opened up, Dumbo flashed his wad. She misunderstood his gesture and his smile.

"You want to have sex, Dumbo?"

Dumbo had not come with that in mind, since no one had ever shown the slightest interest in having sex with him before. But he beamed and blushed at his good fortune.

"Give me your money, Dumbo, and we have sex," Mookie said.

"All right, Kevin, that's enough," Hester said.

"Dumbo started taking off his pants," Kevin said, "and Mookie said, leave your pants on Dumbo."

"Kill it, Kevin!" Maggie said.

"Mookie, she pulls her skirt up and she says, 'See that thing there, Dumbo?'"

"Get yourself another piece of cake and stuff your big mouth before I do it for you," Maggie said.

"So Dumbo, he..."

"Gonna snatch you baldheaded, Kevin!"

Mzz Homer's eyes were scanning the bubble-filled twilight over the front lawn. Mzz Grant was struggling to contain laughter.

Hester threw an empty soda can at Kevin. He ducked.

Two old cars—a panel station wagon with big spots of rust on the side, and Ketchup Robinson's yellow Chevette—came down the hill on Jackson and turned into Oak. The cars parked along the curb in front of Mookie's house, and a host of the rooming house regulars arrested last weekend at Tyrone's piled out of the cars: Tyrone, Mike, the blubbery white Billy, Midnight Marvin, Snothead, the guy from Detroit, Shorty, and Slim.

Kevin jumped off Maggie's porch and went out to the roadway. "Hey, looky, looky, the jailbirds is free!"

"Hey, Yellow Dog, what's happenin', man?" said Midnight Marvin. They exchanged high-fives.

Mike opened the back of the station wagon and withdrew a barbecue grill which he set up on the sidewalk in front of Mookie's house. Shorty took a case of malt liquor from the trunk of the Chevette and placed it on the curb near the barbecue grill. Tyrone, lunging about awkwardly with a roll of masking tape in one hand, attached to the legs of the grill a crude hand-lettered sign:

> CATCH THE SNITCH PARTY

Billy emptied charcoal briquets into the grill and doused them with lighter fluid. Ketchup Robinson struck a match, which flared briefly beneath his Van Dyke beard, showing off to advantage a fiendish smile.

These preparations concluded, the newcomers popped open cans of malt liquor, lit up joints, and stood in a line along the curb gazing toward the party across the street. The silence was that of the cinematic Western frontier town's main drag just before the climactic shoot-out.

Kevin, aware belatedly of the ambiguities, stood in the middle of the street looking from Maggie's party to the one across the street, and back to Maggie's.

Midnight Marvin tried to sound out the syllables in the children's banner: "Use…cock…and lost…yo…"

And now there were other sounds, distant ones—car motors racing, the squeal of tires negotiating a turn at rapid speed, the crack-crack of a handgun, like two broom handles snapped in rapid succession. The sounds seemed to be coming our way.

Maggie leapt from her porch into the yard. "Get your butts in here!" she yelled to her children.

But the children clustered around Barrels of Bubbles, and seated on bikes and trikes, seemed immobilized by the sounds.

An old black funeral hearse with a cockeyed front bumper, and no grill over its radiator, lurched around the corner at Oak and Pickett on mushy shock absorbers and came galumphing toward us.

Crack! I saw the spark of the bullet, and heard its whine, as it ricocheted off the pavement in front of Maggie's house. A white sports car with an open top was following the hearse. A white man with a big stomach and a ponytail stood up on the passenger's side of the sports car. He clung to the windshield with one hand while, with the other, aiming his gun at the hearse.

"Hit the deck!" Maggie yelped, throwing herself face down in the lawn.

Hester and some of the party guests on the porch ducked behind the wainscot. I kept my eyes just above it. The hearse, in an evasive maneuver, rode up over the curb in front of Mookie's house, hit the drug crowds' barbecue grill, flinging charcoal and hot dogs into the air, and smashed the case of malt liquor that exploded in fizzings and geysers.

The two vehicles swung around the corner and rushed up Jackson past our house.

Crack, crack.

Police sirens wailed in the distance.

The two parties dissolved.

13

I WAS ON THE SIDE PORCH OF MY HOUSE toward eleven o'clock after Maggie's party when I heard footsteps in the side yard.

"Illegal trespasser on your property," Mike said from the darkness below. "Better call 911, lock him up."

He went around to the front of the house, onto the porch there, and knocked on the door. "Anybody home?... Trick o' treat!"

I hesitated before opening the door. But I did.

"Catch any lead?" he said.

"No."

"Better luck next time."

I laughed. "The showdown at OK Corral."

"Yeah."

"Who were those guys?"

"Nobody ever seen 'em before."

"Just passing through?"

"I guess."

I stepped out onto the porch. Mike sat down on the porch railing.

"Like to have me that hearse. Put some big speakers in it."

"Dada DOOOOM! Dada DOOOOOM!"

"Yeah, that the one."

A difficult silence.

"Well," he said, "I got outta jail."

"So I see."

"Don't suppose you had anything to do with me being in there?"

"Would I tell you if I did?"

"I don't know what you're gonna do.... I thought you was my friend."

"How was jail?"

"Had air conditioning."

"Beats the rooming house this time of year."

"Yeah....I seen some old friends. About half the football team from my high school was in there. Shark come in yesterday."

"Maggie made a citizen's arrest on him for stealing her pushcart."

"Boy ain't got the brains he was born with....You wanna finish up the story of my suicide?"

I hesitated. A stratagem?

"OK," I said. "As I recall I already paid you for the last installment."

"I know that. I gotta conscience—unlike some other folks I know."

We settled down on the side porch, he on the swing, I in the canvas chair by the table lamp.

"Let's see," I said, "we left off when Yvonne had told you she was too scared to put out. She was trying to send you across the street to Delores."

"Yeah."

"Did you go?"

"Nah, too late by then. I was tired and depressed. Too pooped to pop. Just wanted to go home, forget the whole thing."

He started walking the three miles back to Grant Park. A kid was selling blow on a street corner. Mike still had a few dollars left. He thought he might as well smoke a little on the way home. But when he reached into his pocket for his wallet, it was gone. Yvonne, sitting on his lap, must have picked his pocket. He walked on.

He had reached Boulevard south of Grant Park when a police cruiser on the far side of the street passed by him slowly, then made a U-turn and came back toward him. The cruiser's spotlight came on and shone in Mike's face. The cop got out of the car and started toward him. Mike guessed what had happened: John Reed's business address was on the title to the truck. Marco the mechanic had called John, who had called the police. No sense prolonging the agony. Mike threw up his arms in surrender.

"I don't know what I'm gonna do, officer! I hocked the boss man's truck, and spent all the money on dope and wine—and a piece o' tail I never did get. Now I ain't got no rent money, I'm good as homeless, and nobody ever trust me again. I'm a menace to society. Lock me up." He held his hands pressed together out in front of him, closed his eyes, and waited for cold steel to clamp around his wrists.

But it didn't.

"Well, son," the officer said, "sounds like you got all kinda problems."

"All I really wanted was a little piece o' tail. Was that too much to ask?"

The officer chuckled. "Well now, a little piece of tail's as much as any man wants, but you gotta be careful. Piece o' tail can get a man in a whole lot of trouble."

"Tell me about it!"

"It's like that squirrel," the cop said. "Had a nice fluffy tail on him. Well, one day he raced Amtrak, and lost that pretty tail. Train cut it clean off. Wouldn't been so bad by itself, but he was so proud of that tail, he looked around, and lost his head, too! Point being, man don't want to lose his head over no piece o' tail."

"I'm just a dumb nigger, no good for nothin'."

"Now I don't like to hear no man talking about himself like that," the officer said, "All of us is good for somethin'. You gotta trade?"

"Repair cars."

"Well, there you go. If you can fix cars, you got it made. City's always lookin' for guys to work on patrol cars. I'll put in a good word for you down to the garage, if you want."

"Just lock me up and be done with it," Mike said.

"Son, I can't do that. Reason I stopped just now, we're looking' for a guy raped a woman over in Boulevard Heights."

"Sure as hell wasn't me."

"I know it wasn't you. That's why I gotta keep lookin'… I couldn't take you to jail even if I wanted to. Fulton County Jail's full up tonight. If you need a place to stay, you might go down to East Point, tell them what you done. You know, make it sound like you done it down there....They got a nice new jail. I think they got openings."

The officer got back into his car and drove off.

The ink in my ballpoint pen ceased flowing. I went into the house to get another pen.

"So the cop left, and then what did you do?" I asked, returning to the porch.

"Had me a little talk with Satan."

"How do you mean?"

"Talked to him."

"The way you and I talk?"

"Yeah."

"That happen a lot?"

"Yeah."

"You actually hear a voice?"

"Hear three. Three different angels."

"Do they sound like anyone you know?"

"Nah."

"What do they say?"

"Well.... Satan, he might say, 'You see that icepick over there? Why don't you stick it in that man's head?' And the Good Angel, he say, 'Don't even think about it!'"

"What about angel three?"

"He kind of in-between the other two. He say, 'You could stick that man in the head and get away with it, if you be real careful. But don't mess up.'"

I laughed at the angelic casuistry. "So what did Satan have to say that night?"

"Say, 'Michael, ain't nobody going to help you noway. You're gonna have to help yourself.' I said, 'OK, what should I do?' He say, 'Michael, you put up with a whole lot of shit.' I said, 'Yessir, I do.' He say, 'I would recommend you kill yourself.' I say, 'Good idea. How should I do it?' He say, 'Well, the sure way is put a bullet in your head.' Too messy, I told him. Mumma find me and be upset. Satan say, 'How you wanna do it, then?' I told him I slit my wrists."

"What did Satan say to that?"

"Say, 'That cool.'"

Mike walked the rest of the way up Boulevard to Tyrone's rooming house. As he entered his room Susie, fully clothed, lay on his bed asleep. The table lamp at bedside was burning. Her eyes opened as he shut the door.

"Had your dinner, sweetie?"

"No."

"I make you a plate."

"Don't want no plate."

"You seen me with Damon, didn't you?"

He shrugged his shoulders indifferently. She arose from the bed. Walking past him, she touched his arm. "Gonna make you a plate."

He pulled his carpet bag of tools from under the bed and located in it a dispenser of single-edged razor blades. Withdrawing one blade, he removed its wrapper and sat looking at it glowing dully in the lamplight at bedside. He used these blades all the time in his work to cut hoses. But this one was uniquely interesting.

"Go ahead," Satan said.

"Don't even think about it," said the Good Angel.

He made an incision in his left wrist which did not yield very interesting results. Nothing he had done that night had. He made a second, harder cut in the same place, equally ineffective. But the third cut produced a nice smooth flow of blood. Now we're getting somewhere, he thought.

He lay down and slung his arm over the side of the bed, thinking that might assist gravity. In a few minutes a pool of blood about a yard in diameter had formed on the dark pine floor.

Susie opened the door. "Your plate ready," she said. "Why your arm hang down like that?"

She crossed the room. "What you gone and done, you crazy fool?" She ran from the room. "Call 911! call 911!"

Mike thought it would be interesting to see if his bleeding wrist could serve as a writing instrument. Getting to his feet, he held his arm out in front of him and made a big script "M" on the floor. But the effort required, and his loss of blood, made him dizzy. He lay down again. The pool of blood at bedside was expanding nicely. He was beginning to feel cold, now. He figured by the time the emergency crew arrived, he would be gone.

But Susie had called not only 911, but Mike's mother, who lived nearby. Mama came storming into the room. "What get into you make you do sumpin crazy like that, boy!? Ain't you gotta lick o' sense? Get your black butt off that bed and in my car, we're going to Grady!"

With Susie's help, Mama got him to his feet. Leaning on the two women, Mike made his way down the corridor of the rooming house. By the time they reached Grady's emergency room, he had bled all over the front seat of Mama's Cadillac.

The emergency room doctor sewed him up and gave him a blood transfusion. Two interns helped him into a wheel chair with straps for the arms and legs, and one intern strapped Mike in.

"What's that for?" Mike asked.

"For yo protection," said the intern.

Grady kept him for observation several days, then sent him on to a state mental hospital in DeKalb County where he had his encounters with Thrash Gordon and the crazy people.

While he was there, his mother arranged with Marco the mechanic to have John Reed's truck returned. John himself came to the hospital to visit Mike. When Mike told him what had happened, John said had he been in Mike's shoes, he might have done the same thing. He forgave him and promised more repair work in the future.

Leaving the hospital, Mike told his mother he would need financial help until his car repair business was up and running again, and she gave him a piggy bank the size of a Thanksgiving turkey in which she had been dropping quarters for years.

"Ever thought about suicide since?" I asked Mike, laying aside my pen and paper.

"Now and then. It's been a hard life. Ain't over yet, neither."

I was about to say, every life is hard in its own way—which I thought was the truth—but the words stuck in my mouth. What I did say was, "Well, it ain't over until the fat lady sings. And your story has a happy ending."

"Yeah. Could you tip a guy five for telling you a story with a happy ending?"

I smiled ruefully, and dug into my pocket.

"You still going to give me your old car?"

"Sure, if you want it."

"Yeah, I take it."

Things were getting back to normal.

"Had a dream about that car while I was in jail. I was coastin' it down the hill there in front your house. When I let out the clutch, she started right up. Run like a top! You was running down the hill behind me, hollering, 'I don't want to give it to you now! I don't want to give it to you now!'"

"But you kept on going?"

"Yeah, man, I was movin' right along!" Mike grinned. Br'er Rabbit had one-upped Br'er Fox again.

We laughed at each other together.

Glad Day Publishing Collaborative

(After an engraving by William Blake)

Book publishing is now in the hands of a few media conglomerates whose concern is not books, certainly not with literature or social change. With the elimination of independent bookstores and distribution through the chains the promotional lifetime of a book may now be measured in weeks.

Our particular purpose is to bridge the gap between imaginative literature and political articles and criticism which have been fixed under the labels of "Fiction" and "Non-fiction." But the split has diminished literature and its usefulness to society. With these constraints writers find themselves engaged in self-censorship that has to do both with artistic and formal considerations and with what can be said.

James Gallant's stories and essays have appeared in *The Georgia Review, North American Review, Exquisite Corpse, Raritan, Massachusetts Review, StoryQuarterly,* and a host of other national magazines.

Other books published by Glad Day Collaborative:

History and Spirit by Joel Kovel
  An enquiry into the philosophy of liberation.

The Loggers of Warner by Roy Morrison
  Poems

Serious Kissing by Bárbara Selfridge
  Stories

Travels in Altai by Robert Nichols
  Stories

Ecological Investigations: The Web and the Wheel by Roy Morrison
  Speculative essays

A Voyage to New Orleans by Elisé Reclus
  Translated and edited by John Clark and Camille Martin
  An anarchist's impressions of the Old South.

Swords that Shall Not Strike: Poems of Protest and Rebellion
  by Kenneth Rexroth
  Edited, with an introductory essay, by Geoffrey Gardner

To order:

GLAD DAY BOOKS
Enfield Distribution Co.
P.O. Box 699, Enfield, NH 03748

Phone: 603-632-7377
Fax: 603-632-3611

Editorial Office
P.O. Box 112
Thetford, VT 05074

Phone: 802-785-2608

ISBN: 1-930180-09-8